THE TENDERFOOT

ROBERT VAUGHAN

**WOLFPACK
PUBLISHING**
— EST 2013 —

The Tenderfoot
Paperback Edition
Copyright © 2022 Robert Vaughan

Wolfpack Publishing
5130 S. Fort Apache Rd. 215-380
Las Vegas, NV 89148

wolfpackpublishing.com

Paperback ISBN 978-1-63977-955-0
LCCN

THE TENDERFOOT

SOUTHWEST MISSOURI, APRIL 28TH, 1865

Captain Jake Dunford, often called "Big Jake" because of his size, stood with the other officers of "McPike's Raiders," having been summoned to a meeting by Colonel Liam McPike.

"The Yankee payroll will be coming through, mid-morning, tomorrow."

"I wonder how much money it'll be carryin'," one of the men mused.

"Whatever it's carrying, it'll be money for the South, and not the Yankees," McPike said.

THE NEXT MORNING MCPIKE, Big Jake, and the others were waiting alongside the road. Earlier, two holes had been dug in the road approximately twenty yards apart. A keg of gun power was put into each hole, then covered so that, without a close examination, they wouldn't be noticed.

"Colonel, the coach is a' comin'!" one of the men called.

"All right, get ready," McPike ordered.

Narrow channels had been dug in the road, leading from the hidden holes, to the side of the road, and those channels had been filled with gunpowder.

As Jake waited with the others, he could hear the approach of the coach, not only by the squeak and rumble of the coach itself, but also with the jangle of harness and bit, as well as the drum of hoof beats. There was a guard riding on the coach, and two more mounted guards, one riding on either side.

"Now!" McPike called, as the coach passed over the first, covered hole.

There were two men waiting at the end of each of the narrow channels, and they set a flame to the line of gunpowder. Smoke and sparks raced across the road, then two loud explosions occurred, one before, and one behind the coach.

The explosions startled the horses, and the four-horse team pulling the coach came to a halt. One of the men riding alongside the coach was thrown from his horse.

"What the hell!" the driver shouted.

"You men throw up your hands!" McPike called as he and his raiders rose from their concealment on either side of the road.

"Mister, ain't you got the word?" the shotgun guard called down. "The war's over!"

"We've received no such word," McPike said.

"It's been over for two or three weeks now. Lee surrendered to Gen'l Grant."

"The hell you say. There ain't no way Gen'l Lee would surrender to a damn Yankee," Ed said.

"It's true all right, our Colonel got a telegram tellin' us about it," the coach driver said.

"Throw down the money," McPike ordered.

"Didn't you hear what I said? The war's over."

"I don't care, throw down the money."

"But, now that the war's over, that'd be stealin'," the driver insisted.

"It's no different from what we've been doing for nearly five years," McPike said. "You two climb down."

Still protesting, the driver and guard climbed down from the coach.

"Cosell, go up there and get the money," McPike ordered.

Lieutenant Cosell hurried over to the coach and, using the spokes of the front wheel, climbed up onto the driver's box. Looking down into the splash board, he saw a canvas bag.

"Here it is, boys!" he called, holding it out for the others to see.

"Cut the team loose, then set them running. Do the same with the two riders' horses."

With the team cut loose from the coach, and the two riders dismounted, McPike's men began shooting into the air, causing the horses to gallop away.

"You boy's wearin' long johns under your uniforms?" McPike asked.

"Why are you wantin' to know?"

"On account of I wouldn't want you to be plumb naked when you walk into your camp."

"What?" the driver shouted.

"Shuck outta those uniforms, boys. You're goin' to take a walk.

McPike's Raiders consisted of eight men, and they laughed at the sight of the four Yankee soldiers, walking away wearing nothing but their long john underwear.

Cosell opened the canvas bag.

"There's money in here, Colonel. Lots of it," he said.

"If the South really has surrendered, what are we goin' to do with the money?" Jake asked.

"Why, hell, we'll keep it," McPike replied, to the cheers of agreement from the others.

"No," Jake said. He shook his head. "I wasn't an outlaw before the war started, and I don't plan to be one now."

"Me, neither," Ed said. Before the war, Ed Reynolds had worked as a cook on the ranch own by Jake's father. He and Jake had been long time friends, and when Jake went to war, so did Ed.

"That's all right with me," McPike said. "That'll just mean more money for the rest of us."

"Come on, Ed," Jake said. "If the war really is over, I'm ready to go home."

TWO WEEKS LATER, Jake stood over the graves of his mother and father. Behind him were the remains of what had once been his home. The house and barn were piles of charred lumber, the corral fence was down, and not one horse, mule, cow, or even chicken remained upon what, before the war, had been a productive, five-thousand-acre ranch. Jake knew that his parents had been killed by the same Yankee raiders who had burned the ranch.

In addition, he learned that the entire ranch had been seized by the Yankee government for taxes.

"Those low-life Yankee bastards," Ed, said. "We wasn't regular soldiers durin' the war, but at least we never done nothin' like this."

―――――――――――

THE RANCH adjacent to the Dunford Ranch was the Triple Crown Ranch; thirty thousand acres belonging to Jonas Perkins who, during the war, had been a general in the Texas 20th Brigade of Tarrant County. Before the war, he had been one of the largest and most successful ranchers in Texas. But now, Perkins was nearly destitute. His house hadn't been burned, but his herds had been decimated. When Big Jake went to see Perkins, calling on him late one evening, he was struck with melancholy over what he saw. The once-proud rancher, who had ruled over thirty thousand acres of land and fifteen thousand head of cattle, now sat forlornly in a rocking chair, a broken man. The house was in disrepair, the barns were tumbling down and the bunkhouses and fields were empty.

"General?" Big Jake said, tying his horse to a broken hitch rail in front of the General's house. "General Perkins, it's me, Jake Dunford."

"Jake," General Perkins said. He smiled and stood up. "Jake, how nice of you to come visit me. Come up here, have a seat, boy, have a seat."

Jake sat on an empty keg next to Perkins and looked at him. He sighed.

"We paid a terrible price, didn't we, General?"

"Yes," the General said. "But honor is dear, my boy. It is very dear."

"Honor? Is that what it was?"

"Of course."

"Some of us are still paying. Ed and me, for example. There's nothing left of my parents' ranch, and because we rode with McPike's Raiders, there are reward posters out on us. We can't even show ourselves in public. I had to sneak out here to see you when I was sure there was no one else around."

"Jake, I must know," General Perkins said. "The money. Did you keep any of the money you took?"

"I would have hoped you would know me better than to ask that question," he said. He thought of McPike and the others, who had kept the last money they had taken. He started to tell the general about McPike, but decided not to. "No, I didn't keep any of the money."

"I heard that you lost your ranch to taxes. I also know about what happened to Frank and Agnes. I'm sorry about your parents, they were good people."

"Thanks.

"I wish I could do something for you, I really do." He held his hand out, taking in his ranch. "I wish I could put this ranch back the way it was, and your ranch, and the homes and ranches and farms of all the men from the South who gave so much in a losing cause, but I can't."

"It's not right," Jake said. "There's nothing about it that's right."

2

Everywhere Jake looked in Ft. Worth, he saw Yankee soldiers. There were men wearing blue in all the restaurants, saloons, and out on the street. One thing he noticed was that he never saw a Yankee soldier standing alone; they were always in groups of three, or four, or more. At first he wondered why they were always in groups, then he realized that it must be for protection. The Yankee soldiers were frightened they might be set upon by some of the men who had fought for the South.

Jake was having a beer in the Watering Hole Saloon, which had more Yankee soldiers than locals.

"Hey, what do you think about that ranch Briggs has started?" one of the Yankee soldiers asked.

"Briggs? You mean Lieutenant Briggs? I thought he got out of the army," another replied.

"Yeah, he did."

"And not soon enough if you ask me," another of the soldiers said. "How the hell that son of a bitch ever made an officer is beyond me. He doesn't have sense enough to pour piss out of a boot."

"What do you mean he's started a ranch?"

"Just like I'm sayin' he managed to gather up some land that got took for taxes, 'n a bunch of cows, 'n he's started hisself a ranch."

"Yeah, well, you can bet he didn't come about it honest."

That conversation got Jake to thinking, so he went to Ed with his idea, then the two of them returned to see General Perkins.

"General, how many acres of land do you have left?"

"I have about fifteen thousand acres that haven't been taken for taxes," Perkins said, then he added, "But all the land's good for now, is to help hold the world together. I don't even have a milk cow left."

"What if Ed and I gathered a herd? Could we run them here on your grass and water until we could sell them? We could split the profit."

"Where would you get a herd?"

"I've heard of some pretty large carpetbag spreads near here," Jake said. "Most of their cattle came from our herds. I'll just take some of them back."

"Legally, that's cattle rustling," General Perkins warned.

Jake smiled. "I'd as soon have the game as the name," he said.

Three days later Jake and Ed had gathered four more former soldiers, and the six of them called upon the Briggs Ranch. It was just after sunrise, and they rode into a field where there were about five hundred cattle.

"Look here," Ed said. "This is a circle Y brand. This cow came from the Younger Ranch."

"And here's some from the Triple Crown," another said.

"Jake, wasn't the DX your folks' brand?" someone asked.

"Yes."

"Then these here two cows is yours."

"Wrong," Jake said.

"What?"

Jake smiled. "Every steer in this field is ours, so let's get them over to the Triple Crown."

The six men moved into position, then started moving the cattle away from the Briggs Ranch. By mid-afternoon, all the cattle had been taken to the Triple Crown.

By now, there were several new ranches in the area, owned by men who had no previous ranching experience, and who weren't even Texans. These were carpet-baggers, Yankees who had come to Texas to take advantage of an abundance of land and cheap cattle. The cattle and land were both available and cheap, because they had been confiscated as spoils of war. Big Jake, Ed, and four men they had gathered to ride with them, began taking cattle from the carpetbaggers' ranches.

Within two months, there were thirty-five hundred head of cattle, of various brands, in the fields of the Triple Crown Ranch. That many cattle required hands to look after them, so once again, the Triple Crown became a productive ranch, complete with wranglers. The once-empty bunkhouses were opened again, and the Triple Crown was well on its way to returning to its pre-war productivity.

In addition to recovering "confiscated" cattle from the Carpetbagger ranches, they also began "cow hunts" rounding up cattle that had gone astray during the war, when there weren't enough cowboys to look after them.

The carpetbaggers, realizing that their herds were being systematically thinned, complained to the local authorities. But the local sheriffs, deputies, and reconstituted Texas Rangers, realizing that Jake and the others were setting things right by recovering stolen cattle, offered no response to the complaints filed by the carpetbaggers. As a result of the local authorities showing no interest in how Jake and the others were rebuilding their ranches, Yankee carpetbaggers formed a cattlemen's association, and established a cattlemen's enforcement agency. The enforcement agency members were appointed as special U.S. Deputies, which gave them the authority to investigate what they considered to be cattle thieves.

One afternoon Jake, Ed, and Abe Johnson, were driving a string of fifteen beeves that had been re-acquired from a carpet bagger. What was significant about these cows, was that every one of them bore the brand of the Rocking J, which was Abe Johnson's brand.

"Looks like we've got some visitors comin' our way," Abe said, nodding toward four men who were riding toward them.

"Association deputies, you reckon?" Ed asked.

"More 'n likely," Jake agreed.

As the four men approached, Jake saw that all four were holding guns.

"Where are you boys goin' with them stoled cows?" one of the deputies asked.

"You're right, they are stolen, but they were stolen from me," Abe said. "I'm just takin' 'em back home now. If you'll look, you'll see that they all have my brand."

"That don't matter none, they was legal confiscated,"

one of the deputies said. "So if you got 'em, that makes 'em stoled."

"We can take it to court," Jake said. "I think the court will see it our way."

"You're right, a Texas court prob'ly would, which is why we'll just hold the court right here."

The deputy who spoke pulled the trigger, and Abe was shot out of his saddle.

"What the hell!" Ed shouted.

Jake and Ed drew their own pistols then, and in the exchange of fire, Jake had his horse shot out from under him. But, in that same exchange of fire, all four deputies were killed.

Neither Jake nor Ed was hit, but Abe was killed.

"The sons of bitches," Ed said. "Me 'n Abe had been friends since we was kids."

"I DON'T THINK it'll be safe for you two boys to stay here any longer. I think you should go somewhere else," Perkins said when they reached the Triple Crown and told him what happened.

"And just where would that be?"

"Arizona," Perkins suggested.

"What?"

"You should go to Arizona. There won't be anyone out there who's ever heard of either one of you."

"What about my cattle? I can't drive them all the way to Arizona," Jake said.

"I'll give you fifteen hundred dollars for your cattle," Perkins offered. "I know they're worth more than that, but that's all I can afford."

"Well, it's better than just leaving them here," Jake said.

"Eagle Canyon," Perkins suggested.

"What's that?"

"It's a place somewhere in Northern Arizona, near the San Francisco Mountains. Once you get there, look for the Turquoise Ranch. You shouldn't have any trouble finding it. Curly says it's the biggest ranch in Arizona."

"Curly?"

"Yeah, Curly Stevens. Remember him?"

"Yes, he used to work for you."

"I'll write a letter for you to give him."

IT TOOK Jake and Ed just under a month to reach Arizona. Once they arrived, they were on the southern margin of the Colorado Plateau, which offered an exceptional variety of geologic wonders. The landscape of the plateau was composed of the towering, glaciated peaks of the San Francisco Mountains, underground lava tubes and blowholes; meteor-blasted Barringer Crater, and cinder cones and lava flows of the San Francisco volcanic field. It was here, that they believed they would find Turquoise Ranch.

Their horses were travel worn and tired as Jake and Ed rode on down the trail toward the town that they hoped was just over the next rise, or perhaps beyond the next hill.

It was four more hills before a town was encountered, if the place could be called a town. There were only two streets, and they formed an *X*, with the bulk of the buildings near the crossroad. The buildings were low and rough wood, though several of them had wooden fronts which rose higher than the buildings themselves. A raised, wooden sidewalk graced both sides of the street for the length of the nicer of the buildings, but after a short distance, the sidewalk ended, and there was nothing but a small dirt path in front of the shabbier buildings. The biggest and most prominent structure was a saloon, identified by the sign painted on front as "The Gilded Cage."

"Well, I reckon that's as good a place as any for a fella to get a plate full of beans and somethin' to cut this dust," Ed suggested.

Jake agreed, and the two men tied their horses off in front of the building and went inside.

There were more than a dozen men inside, and they looked up with unbridled curiosity as Jake and Ed entered. In a town this remote, no stranger went unnoticed. The bartender came over and passed a damp rag across the bar in front of them.

"What'll it be?" he asked. That was the only question voiced, but his eyes asked volumes.

"Whiskey, 'n a little grub, if you serve vittles here," Jake said.

"Beans," the bartender said. "With a hot pepper for seasonin'."

"Sounds mighty fine," Jake agreed.

There was a sudden fanfare of guitar music, and Jake and Ed turned to see a Mexican man sitting on a stool, holding a guitar. A moment later a very pretty young woman came out, and began a flamenco dance to the young man's accompaniment.

"Well now," Ed said, smiling. "I'd say this is a right friendly little town, to set up a welcome like this for us."

The girl proved to be even more friendly, for after her dance, she answered Ed's smile and came to sit with the two men. Her name was Angelina, and she was the sister of the guitar player. Ed bought her a drink while Jake obligingly offered to take care of the horses.

It was then that Jake saw Maggie for the first time. It was also nearly the last time, for Maggie and an older man who was with her were standing near the wall of the livery stable with their hands raised. Two masked men were holding drawn guns on them, and one of the gunmen was relieving Maggie's companion of his wallet.

"Ha," the gunman who had just taken the wallet said. "What did I tell you? He just sold five hunnert head of cattle. I know'd he'd be carryin' a fat wallet."

"That's not my money," the robbery victim said. "That belongs to Mr. Edward Baker, and the brand."

"Wrong," the robber said with a laugh. "It belongs to us now."

"I know who you two men are," Maggie said. "You're Froggie Dolan, and you're Augie Phillips. Papa, you remember. They're the two who ran off last year. They stole a couple of horses, too, if I recall."

"Augie, what the hell?" one of the gunmen said, and it was clear by the expression in his voice that her recognition had disturbed him. "She knows who we are!"

"Shut up, you damn fool!" Augie replied. His voice, like that of his companion, was muffled by the hood he wore over his head.

"I see you aren't much better at robbing than you were at punchin' cattle," the girl's father said.

"You know the trouble with you two? You got too good 'a memory, and too big a mouth. We're gonna have to kill the both of you."

"No, I don't think you will," Jake called. He had waited until now to make his presence known, just to make certain that things were what they seemed to be.

"Augie, shoot 'im!" Froggie yelled, and both robbers turned toward Jake with their guns blazing, but Jake had already pulled his gun before he challenged them, and he stood there as the two men shot wildly, returning their fire with deadly accuracy. Both men fell to his bullets.

"Are you two all right?" Jake asked, holstering his pistol after the two men were down.

"Yes, thanks to you," the older man said. He smiled and extended his hand. "My name is Abel Cole, mister. This here is my daughter, Maggie. I don't know that I've ever seen better shooting."

"The name is Jake Dunford, and I got lucky, that's all," Jake said.

"No, sir. We're the ones who got lucky when you came along. Tell me, Mr. Dunford. Is there anything I can do for you? I'm sure Mr. Baker would like to reward you for what you did here."

"Mr. Baker?"

"Clyde Baker. He's the manager of the Turquoise Ranch. I'm his foreman."

Jake smiled. "Well now this is a lucky break. My partner and I came here looking to get a job with the Turquoise Ranch. Do you know Curly Stevens?"

"Yes, of course I know Curly. He's a good hand."

"We have a letter to Curly from a mutual friend. We were going to ask Curly to get us on with the ranch."

"You know anything about cattle?"

Jake smiled. "We're from Texas."

Abel Cole laughed. "I reckon that's recommendation enough for me. Where is your pard now?"

"He's tied up for the moment," Jake said, smiling and looking at Maggie really closely for the first time. What a beautiful girl she was.

"Miss, you wouldn't be married or anything, would you?" he asked, tipping his hat politely to her.

"Married?" Maggie replied. She smiled. "No, Mr. Dunford, I'm not married."

"Engaged, or spoken for?"

Maggie laughed. "No, I'm not spoken for, either. I'm my own woman, Mr. Dunford."

"That's good," Jake said. "That's real good."

Jake decided then and there that this was the woman he was going to marry.

3

TWENTY YEARS LATER

J ake stood looking down at the graves of Maggie and her father. Maggie had died of meningitis nine years earlier, leaving Jake with a ten-year-old daughter, Melanie. Cole had died a year before Maggie, at which time Theodore Baker had appointed Jake as foreman of the Turquoise Ranch.

When Theodore retired, he attempted to get Jake appointed to take his place as ranch manager, but was unable to do so.

"Morgan, Trevathan, and Daigh want a lawyer," Theodore said. "I'm sorry, I tried to get them to hire you as the manager. I would have gone directly to the owner... if I had any idea who the owner was."

"It's hard to believe that, after all these years, nobody actually knows who owns Turquoise," Jake had said.

"I'm not sure anyone owns it," Theodore said. "I mean, any one person. Morgan, Trevathan, and Daigh is a legal firm, which is why they use a manager. I don't know why they've decided now that they want a lawyer as manager. Hell, I'm not a lawyer, and I've managed the ranch for more 'n twenty years."

Thus it was that, for the last year Les Garrison, a lawyer from Denver, had been manager of Turquoise Ranch, and the fifteen thousand head of cattle encompassed on the thirty thousand acres of well-watered grassland that made up the ranch.

"I thought I might find you out here with mama and grandpa."

Jake turned to see his daughter, Melanie, now a beautiful twenty-year-old young woman.

"Hello, darlin', what do you need?" Jake asked.

"Les wants to see you."

"He's not in my office, is he?"

Melanie smiled. "No, Papa, I know better than that. He's waiting in the parlor."

Jake and Melanie lived in the foreman's house, which was a nice house with a parlor, dining room, kitchen, a small office, and two bedrooms. The biggest house on the ranch would be where the owner would live, if there had been an owner in residence. Jake and the fifteen men who worked on the Turquoise, called it the 'Big House.' And because there was no resident owner, that house was currently occupied by Les Garrison, the ranch manager.

Les Garrison was a handsome man, and quite vain about it. Whereas everyone else on the ranch wore denims and linsey-woolsey shirts, Garrison often wore a suit, a white shirt, and a silver and turquoise bolo tie.

"What can I do for you, Les?" Jake asked.

"Is it true, that you fired Woods and Peevey?" Garrison asked.

"Yes."

"Why?"

"They aren't holding up their end of the work load," Jake said.

"What do you mean?"

"I mean that when they are supposed to be working with some of the other men, they're letting the other men do all of the work."

"Here's the thing, Jake. I hired Woods and Peevey, and that means only I can fire them."

"All right, then you fire them."

"I don't think so. I hired them for a special reason, and stringing fence wire isn't that reason. From now on, I will be assigning them their jobs."

"You're the boss," Jake said.

Garrison sighed, and shook his head. "Jake, you're a good foreman, and I've no wish for us to be at odds with one another. Especially as I hope to be a part of your family one day. I can understand why you might be displeased with Woods and Peevey if you didn't realize I had hired them for a special job."

"What job have you hired them for?" Jake asked.

Garrison smiled. "It has to do with the owners. I'm not sure they want it known. It's a matter of marketing competition and that sort of thing. Let's just say it's why they thought it would be best to hire an attorney as their ranch manager."

"The owners?"

"One can only suppose so. As you know, I deal only with the legal firm that represents the owners."

"All right, I'll have no more dealings with Woods and Peevey. As far as I'm concerned, they aren't even a part of the cowhands, they work just for you."

"Good," Garrison said, "and Jake, I know you were only doing what you thought was best, so please don't look at this as some sort of reprimand. When I was hired, Theodore Baker told me you were the best ranch foreman in Arizona, and I'm certainly inclined to agree with him." Garrison extended his hand. "I hope there are no hard feelings."

Jake took Garrison's hand.

"No hard feelings," he said.

BOSTON HARBOR, APRIL, 1886

Robert Barringer stood on the deck of the *Comet,* looking out over the rolling sea and enjoying the sensation of salty sea spray in his face. It wasn't just the sensation of the sea that had brought him out on deck, though. Rob, as he was called, had come here to avoid the unpleasantness in the dining room. His recent announcement had been the cause of the unpleasantness, falling upon the others like a bombshell. Rob knew before he said anything that such would be the reaction, but he was determined to go through with his plans, regardless of what anyone said. As it turned out, they had plenty to say, and he had no doubt but that they were still saying it.

Let them talk. His mind was made up. He was leaving home, and he was going out West. Morgan, Trevathan, and Daigh had represented Rob's father. Rob had studied law with the thought he might join the firm as one of their lawyers. However, when Rob's father died, he gave up on that idea, and began thinking about leaving Boston and going out west.

When Rob's father died, he had inherited Turquoise Ranch, a ranch that his father had never seen. For the last few months, Rob had been thinking about going out to the ranch. At first, he had only been thinking about visiting the ranch, but the more he thought of it, the stronger the idea was that he wouldn't just visit the ranch, he would move there.

That was the announcement that was the cause of the earlier discourse.

"What in the world would make you think something like that?" Jason Daigh asked. "You made outstanding grades in law school, you've passed the bar, and we have a place for you in our firm."

"I know, and I appreciate that, very much," Rob said. "But this is something I've been wanting to do for a long time."

"You know your father would have wanted you to join our firm. Besides, he left you with a considerable estate. You are a wealthy man in your own right, Rob, independent of your grandfather. Don't you think you would be better served if you administered your estate from a position within our firm?"

Rob shook his head. "I am wealthy because of my father, not because of anything I have ever done. And this is something I've been dwelling on for a long time, so I have decided to do it."

The yacht on which Rob had come to his decision was the family yacht, the *Comet.* It was a 256-foot-long vessel, used by the Barringers to ferry family and friends not only from Boston to Newport or the Caribbean, but across the Atlantic to their several European residences as well. As a yacht, the boat was magnificent. It could make nineteen knots and carry enough coal to travel over six thousand miles without stopping.

As impressive as its performance, however, was its interior. It looked more like a sea-going mansion than a vessel. It featured high ceilings, skylights, paneled walls and parquet floors. The dining room which Rob had so recently abandoned was exquisitely done in Louis XIV furniture, and set with the finest silver, China, and crystal. It had no less than nine plushly furnished staterooms, plus a grand salon which could easily accommodate one hundred guests.

The *Comet* was operated by a crew of seventy officers and men. That was fifteen less than was required to operate J. P. Morgan's *Corsair,* but that didn't mean that the Barringer vessel was smaller, or less of a yacht. It merely meant that the *Comet* was more up to date, and possessed of all the latest labor-saving devices which enabled it to function with a smaller crew. The *Comet* was every bit as large as the *Corsair,* and certainly no less luxurious in its appointments.

The *Comet* was owned by Rob's grandfather, Andrew K. Barringer, a man who had made millions of dollars in the shipping and railroad industry. The elder Barringer had made all of his money within his lifetime, for he had started life as a poor stable boy, and risen to heights of wealth and power that were the things of dreams. However, despite the fact that Andrew Barringer had fulfilled the American dream and had amassed one of the largest fortunes in the country, he was never fully accepted into "society," because his money was new money, and therefore, "tainted." His money, however, was more than welcome.

It never bothered Andrew to be left out of accepted society, for he was a man at peace with himself. In his own mind, he was still the stable boy who had just happened to get lucky.

But Andrew married Helen Cornelius, a pretty young woman from a family that had a fine old name, though a collapse in fortunes had long ago cost them their wealth. Helen thought that the combination of her family name with Andrew's money would take care of both of them, by restoring her family to its rightful place in society, while elevating Andrew.

Despite Helen's wishes, it didn't work out that way. Her family continued to be regarded as "genteel poor" and Andrew as *nouveau riche.* As a result, Helen had to put all her hopes for regaining social position in Abe, their son. After all, Abe was second-generation money, and a fourth-generation descendant of the Cornelius family, one of the finest old names in New England. Martin Cornelius had been a governor, appointed by the King of England, before the Revolution. He was written about in all the history books because he voluntarily surrendered his governorship in order to accept a commission in the Massachusetts Militia, allying himself with the American cause against the Crown. By being his direct descendant, Abe Barringer's entry into society was all but assured.

In order to prepare him for his station in life, Helen saw to it that Abe was educated in the best schools, met the right people and took the grand tour of Europe. Abe was groomed in every way to assume his rightful position, and Helen even saw to it that Abe married well. But Abe's reign in society was cut tragically short, for he and his wife were killed in a hotel fire in New York, leaving their young son, Rob, to be raised by Helen and Andrew Barringer.

Rob was third-generation money, and a descendant, not only of Helen's illustrious family, but possessed of quite a bit of blue blood on his mother's side as well. Because of that, he was granted automatic membership into the society to which his grandmother had so ardently aspired. But Rob, who had everything handed him, didn't want any of it. He was not only different from his grandmother in that attitude, but was different from the others in his peer group as well. Rob considered the parties, dances, and endless succession of social events boring, and a waste of time. To that degree, he was much more attuned to his grandfather's no-nonsense philosophy of life.

But it wasn't just Rob's attitude which set him apart from the others. In any party or at any home, school, or social gathering, Rob stood out whether he wanted to or not. That was because he was very tall, well over six feet, with broad shoulders, a muscular chest, flat stomach, long arms and great, spreading hands. He had discovered the game of football in college, and though it was considered much too rough a game for those who were born to the gentry, Rob not only played it, he excelled in it. He was big and strong, and both qualities were desirable attributes for playing football, so Rob became somewhat of a sports hero, much to the chagrin of his grandmother and social peers. The game of football broke Rob's nose and that gave his face a rugged look which tended to substantiate the impression of a ruffian that he gave on first meeting.

Rob was aware that his great size and rugged looks set him apart from the others, and he intensified that separation by his attitude.

Despite Rob's desire to avoid what he considered the "waste of excess indulgence," it was impossible for him to avoid everything, so it was that he was more or less forced to go along on the family cruise to the Bahamas.

"We'll sweep down there for a week or two," his grandmother said, "and we'll all have a wonderful time. The Vanderbilts will be there, and so will the Mellons.

Oh, and I'm sure you'll be pleased to know that the Proctor family is going with us. You won't mind that, will you, Rob? After all, Evelyn is such a lovely girl."

Evelyn Proctor *was* a lovely girl, and she and Rob were engaged to be married. Rob wasn't sure how that had come about. He could not recall asking her to marry him. He knew that his grandmother wanted them to get married, for Evelyn was the right girl from the right family, but Rob couldn't recall exactly when it became common knowledge that they were to be married. Now, he found himself trapped into an engagement that wasn't of his making and which he didn't wish to keep. Things were certain to come to a head since he had informed everyone that he intended to go west as soon as they returned. At first the others thought he was teasing, then, when they realized he was serious, they tried to talk him out of it. When the atmosphere in the dining room began to get uncomfortable, Rob just got up and left the dinner table. He had been on deck ever since.

4

Rob was standing at the rail watching the sunset when he became aware of someone behind him. He turned and saw Evelyn Proctor. She was properly dressed in deck whites and canvas shoes, and Rob had to admit that she was devastatingly pretty. She smiled at him, making a brave effort to cover up the fact that she had been crying.

"I've been standing here for a long time," she said. "Didn't you even suspect it?"

"No," Rob replied. "I'm afraid I was thinking about something else."

"Oh, I can believe that. Knowing you, you were probably off in some totally different world, no doubt playing football or something equally as brutal."

"Something like that," Rob admitted, realizing that Evelyn just didn't want to face up to the truth.

Evelyn put her hand gently to Rob's face, and ran her fingers down the bridge of his nose and across the lump formed by the break.

"How awful," she said, screwing her face up distastefully. "That stupid game has disfigured you for life."

Rob laughed. "I never was exactly handsome."

"Perhaps not, but you certainly didn't need to go and make matters worse."

Rob laughed again. "Well, look at it this way. When I leave, you can just say 'good riddance' and go about finding someone else."

"I don't want anyone else," Evelyn pouted. "You know I care only about you."

"Really?"

"Yes, of course."

"Then come West with me." Why did he ask her that, he wondered? He didn't really want her to come with him. Or did he? Perhaps if she did, she would show him more spunk than he gave her credit for.

"Well, I'd be glad to go West for a visit. I think it might even be exciting. We could put your grandfather's private car onto a train and just have a marvelous time. In fact, I think we could get several of our friends to go with us and make it a party. A wonderful, mobile party which would last from Boston to... wherever."

"No," Rob said. "Don't you understand? That is exactly what I don't want. I'm not going for a visit. I'm going out there to live. I am going to move to Arizona."

"Arizona? My God, that's nothing but wilderness—desert and mountain country. Arizona isn't even a state. It's full of wild Indians—what's that Indian's name that everyone has heard about? Jeremy?"

"Geronimo."

"Yes, Geronimo. Why, he is still scalping people, from what I read."

"I think they have him pretty much on the run now," Rob said.

"Rob, you aren't really serious, are you? You don't actually mean that you are going to live out there?"

"Yes," Rob said. "During the war, my father bought a ranch out in the Arizona Territory, believing that beef was going to be at a premium, and he was right, there has been a market for beef. My father never visited the ranch, not even once. It has been administered by Morgan, Trevathan, and Daigh ever since he bought it. But since he died, the ranch passed to me and it has continued to be administered by a trust. But that will be no more, because I'm going to go out to run the place myself."

Evelyn laughed. "You're going to run a ranch? Why in heaven's name would you want to do that? Why, you don't know the first thing about ranching, do you?"

"No," Rob admitted, "but I think I can learn."

"Rob, really, you can't be serious. Please tell me you aren't serious."

"I'm very serious," Rob said, and sighed. "Evelyn, I don't fit in with all the others, and you know it. I know what they say about me... what they call me."

"They don't mean anything by it, Rob. You know how they are. They're just jealous of you, that's all."

"Yes, I know how they are, and I don't want any part of them. They tease me because I'm bigger and stronger than most men. For some reason, they seem to find that amusing. Well, that's all right, I can handle that. But they would tease with equal vigor someone who had a club foot or some other handicap. Don't you see, Evelyn, our friends are wastrels, the lot of them. And I don't want anything to do with them."

"You shouldn't talk about them like that. They *are* your friends, Rob. They are people you were raised with, and they are my friends as well. Why, they are the finest names from the wealthiest families in this country. You should be proud to be a part of them."

"The finest names from the wealthiest families. What did any of us do to become the finest names from the wealthiest families, other than be born?"

"There have always been various stations in life," Evelyn said. "It's just the way things are."

"Yes, well, I don't want any part of it."

"Excuse me, sir, ma'am," a sailor said, walking by at that very moment. He picked up a coil of rope, then returned to the stern of the yacht, so that, once again, Rob and Evelyn were alone in their conversation.

"That was Lou Clancey," Rob said, pointing to the sailor. "I have known him since I was a boy. Would you say he's my friend?"

"No, of course not," Evelyn replied. "Why, he is so far beneath your station that he couldn't possibly be your friend."

"You're right," Rob said. "I would like for him to be my friend." Rob sighed. "But the way things are, he can no more afford to be friends with me than I can to be friends with him. That's the sort of thing I want to get away from. And that's why I'm going out West."

"Rob," Evelyn started, then she let out a sigh. "Rob, I didn't want to say this to you. I didn't want to make it seem that I was trying to bring undue pressure on you. But, if you go West, our engagement is off."

"Yes," Rob said. "I was hoping you would see it that way."

"You were hoping… you mean… you mean you planned to break our engagement?"

"I planned to give you your freedom. This is something I have to do, but it isn't something I feel I can force on anyone else."

"Rob, do you know what you are saying?" Evelyn asked in a weak voice.

"Yes," Rob replied.

Evelyn began to cry softly, and Rob reached out and put his hand on her shoulder.

"Evelyn, you don't really love me and you know it. You have been in love with the *idea* of marrying me, but you haven't been in love with me. There are others... so many others... who are better suited to you. You'll find someone else soon. I know you will."

Abruptly Evelyn's tears of sorrow turned to tears of anger.

"When I do find another, you can bet he won't be a big, ugly ape like you!" she said angrily.

"I'm sure he won't be," Rob replied gently, and the gentleness of his reply seemed to anger Evelyn all the more.

"Oh, I hate you!" Evelyn lashed out, and she started hitting him.

Rob stood there, letting her rain blows on him until she grew tired and frustrated, and finally, with another choked sob, she turned and ran away, disappearing through a hatch that led into the grand salon of the yacht.

Rob turned back toward the sea. The sun had set, but the sky still wasn't dark. The sea looked slate gray under the dim twilight. He watched it in silence for several moments.

"I just saw Evelyn," a voice said from behind him. The voice was that of his grandfather, and Rob turned to see the old man, perfectly dressed in a blue blazer and white pants. The older man was wearing an ascot and smoking a pipe. He was playing the society game, and he knew it. When Rob was younger, he used to be embarrassed by his grandfather's role-playing. Then he learned that his grandfather was, in his own way, having his fun with the ultra-rich. He affected their mannerisms, not out of any desire to become one of them, but in a life-long parody of their actions. It was his way of ridiculing them, though his ridicule was so subtle that very few realized what he was doing. When Rob finally did realize it, and mentioned it to his grandfather, he and his grandfather had a wonderful laugh, and the older man seemed genuinely glad that someone else was finally able to share the joke with him. From that moment on, Rob and his grandfather had been exceptionally close.

"I imagine she told you that our engagement is off," Rob said.

"Yes," Andrew replied, sucking on his pipe. "She told me."

"Well?" Rob said.

"Well, what?"

"How do you feel about it?"

Andrew chuckled. "Makes no difference how I feel. The question is, how do you feel about it?"

"I..." Rob started, then he sighed and was silent for a moment.

"What is it?" Andrew asked.

"I'm ashamed to say it, Grandpa, but the only thing I can feel at the moment is a sense of relief."

"Evelyn is a lovely young woman," Andrew said.

"Yes, I know she is," Rob admitted.

"She has a lot of good qualities."

"Yes, I'm sure of that, too."

"But you had no business being engaged to her in the first place."

Rob looked at his grandfather and smiled.

"Thanks," he said. "I was hoping someone could see it

my way. Now, if I could just convince everyone that I am not crazy for wanting to go to Arizona."

"I don't think you're crazy," Andrew said. "If you want to go, go ahead. I think it would be good for you."

"Do you really feel that way?"

"Yes," Andrew said. "That is, if you have the courage to do it right."

"Do it right? What do you mean?"

"You are planning on going out there to take over and run your ranch, right?"

"Yes."

"What do you know about ranching?"

Rob laughed. "You sound like Evelyn. She asked me the same thing."

"Then she asked you a good question. What do you know about running a ranch?"

"I don't know anything about it. I'll admit that."

"Then I think you ought to start a little lower."

"What do you mean?"

"Go out there and go to your ranch. Work on it if you must. But don't go out there ready to take over. Tell the manager and the foreman that you want to work on the ranch as a hand for a while. That way, you'll learn it from the bottom up."

"You mean, just work as a hand?" Rob asked.

"Yes."

"That's an idea," he said. "I'll have to think about it."

"Of course, you will," Andrew said. "I'm the first to admit that it doesn't have all that pleasant a sound to it. It will take courage. But you'll learn more that way than by just going out and taking over."

Rob was silent for a moment, then he smiled. "I know an even better way to learn," he said.

"What's that?"

"I'll go out there and work on the ranch, all right. But I won't tell them who I am. I'll simply take the job as a hired hand."

Andrew chuckled. "Now you're putting yourself to the real test," he said. "Are you sure you want to do that?"

"I'm absolutely positive," Rob said.

"Maybe you should tell either the manager or the foreman," Andrew suggested.

"No, I don't want to tell a soul."

Andrew said, "If you go out the way you are saying, it's going to look as if you're spying on the people you have running the ranch for you."

"Well, if they're honest, they have nothing to fear," Rob said. "If they're dishonest, then maybe a little spying wouldn't hurt."

"All right, boy," Andrew said. "It's your ranch; you have the right to run it any way you see fit." Andrew smiled broadly and ran his hand through his thin white hair. "I've only got one thing to say."

"What's that, Grandfather?"

"I wish it were forty years ago, and it was me instead of you going out there. You're going to have a fine adventure, boy. A very fine adventure. And anyone who can't see that, or the reason for your going, is a damn fool. Rob, if no one else in the whole world can understand why you're going, I can and you have my blessings."

"Thanks, Grandpa," Rob said. "It means a lot to me to know that I haven't been totally ostracized."

"I would offer you my private car for the trip, but I think making an entrance like that would make it impossible for you to just sneak in without anyone knowing who you are."

"Grandpa, you'll see to it that nobody back here lets anybody out there in on my secret, won't you?"

"Yes, but the only people here who actually have any contact with the ranch are the ones at Morgan, Trevathan, and Daigh. It might be a good idea if before you go, you visit with them to make certain that your secret is kept, until you want it known. Then, when the time comes, you can use them to let it be known that you are actually the owner, and not just a hired hand."

"Well, I'll just tell them when the time comes."

Rob's grandfather chuckled. "And they'll believe you? Think about it, Rob. You're in the bunkhouse with the other men and you decide to say, "Guess what, guys, I own Turquoise."

Rob laughed as well. "You're right. I'll need some validation."

5

J ason Daigh sighed, then poured wine for Rob and himself. They were in Daigh's private office.

"So, you haven't changed your mind, have you?"

"No, sir, I'm going to Arizona, and I'm going to work on Turquoise."

"As a common ranch hand, and you don't want anyone to know who you are?"

"Right."

"Well, Les Garrison is the ranch manager, and he is actually the only one we do business with. We have purposely kept him in the dark as to who owns the ranch, and he thinks it's in a blind trust. So, there won't be any problem keeping your secret, as we are already set up to do so."

"Thank you."

"When, and how, are you going to make your ownership of the ranch known?"

"I don't know. Grandpa suggested that you might establish my ownership when I'm ready."

Daigh nodded. "We'll be most pleased to do so. When

you are ready to claim ownership, have a lawyer send us a telegram, and we'll validate it for you."

"Yes, that would work. But, what if…"

"What if what?"

"What if someone else contacts you, claiming to be me?"

Daigh smiled. "We'll use a password," he suggested.

TWO DAYS LATER, Rob and his grandfather went by the elder Barringer's private carriage to the Boston and Maine Depot.

"Gordon, we will be here for some time," Andrew said to the driver. "If you would like, you can park the carriage, then step into the depot restaurant for coffee or something."

"Thanks, Mr. Barringer," the driver said.

"How will you be travelling?" Andrew asked his grandson as the two of them approached the ticket counter.

"I've studied the trip on railroad maps," Rob said. "I will be passing through Massachusetts, New York, Pennsylvania, Ohio, Indiana, Illinois, Missouri, Indian Territory, Texas, New Mexico, and finally into Arizona. I'll have to make several changes of trains and railroads, and it's going to last for ten days. So, because of that, I'm going to go by Pullman car. That way, I won't be totally exhausted when I arrive in Flagstaff."

"May I make a suggestion?" Andrew asked.

"Yes, of course."

"If you don't want people to know who you are, arrive by day coach."

"But grandpa…"

Andrew held up his hand to halt Rob in mid-comment. "I said arrive by day coach. You can ride in comfort until you change trains in Albuquerque. From there, you should ride in a day coach for your last day."

Rob smiled. "Yes, Grandpa, I will. That's a great suggestion, thank you."

Andrew chuckled. "Let's see if you still thank me after spending several hours in a day coach."

Rob bought the tickets he would need for the passage, and his grandfather waited in the depot with him, until his train was called.

"You know, Rob, I wish I was 40 years younger. I would be going with you. You're going to have a grand adventure."

"I must say that I am very much looking forward to it," Rob replied.

"Here comes the train," someone called, though no announcement was necessary as everyone could hear the puffing steam. The engineer rang the bell as the train drew closer, then, with sound of steel on steel, and the compression of the couplings, they train came to a stop. Shortly after it did so, the conductor stepped down, as several arriving passengers left the train.

The conductor looked at his stop watch, then bellowed, "All aboard!"

Rob boarded the train, then looked through the window to wave goodbye to his grandfather.

A grand adventure, he thought as the train pulled out of the station. He smiled. *Yes, I think it will be.*

BECAUSE HE BEGAN his trip by Pullman car, the nights were passed comfortably in pull-down bunks. He was enjoying the long trip, and particularly enjoying his interaction with the other passengers. They were much more down to earth than the people he had been associating with back in Boston, and he appreciated the experiences.

Nine days into the trip, he changed accommodations in Albuquerque, as planned. A few hours after leaving Albuquerque though, he encountered an event he would just as well not have experienced. The train had stopped for water, when several men came aboard, all of them armed. They passed through the cars taking money from the passengers.

"All right," the train robber who had come into Rob's car shouted, "just pretend that you're in church, 'n when I pass down the aisle, you put all your money in this bag I'm carryin.'"

Frightened, everyone in train car began responding to his order, until he reached Rob's seat. When held the sack out to Rob, Rob just stared at him.

"Come along, mister, drop your money in just like ever' one else has." He emphasized his demand by thrusting the gun closer to Rob. That was just what Rob was waiting for, and he grabbed the gun, holding his hand on the cylinder so that it couldn't move, making it impossible for the robber to pull the trigger. With his inert gun in one hand, and the money sack in his other hand, the robber was unable to defend himself against a sharp punch to his chin, which knocked him out. Then, Rob got up from his seat and dragged the, now unconscious, robber onto the vestibule where he tossed him out. The robber fell hard onto the gravel ballast, then slid down the berm to the bottom. When Rob came back into the car, everyone was looking at him in shock.

"Blackie! Blackie, come on out now, we're goin'!" someone called from outside the train.

By now three of the men in Rob's car pulled their own guns, raised the windows, and began firing at the train robbers, who, except for the man Rob and thrown out, were now all mounted. When the shooting started, the outlaws rode away.

"Mister, that was some trick you done," one of the three armed passengers said.

"I didn't want to give him any of my money," Rob said, and the others laughed.

The man who had spoken to him picked up the bag the robber had been carrying. "Yeah, well, I don't reckon any of us wanted that either. Okay folks, I'm going to pass back down the aisle, and you can reach in and get your money back."

When the train stopped at the next depot, the sheriff and a deputy came through the cars, interviewing all the passengers, trying to get as much information as they could as to the identity of the robbers. When they reached the car Rob was in, the other passengers all bragged on him, explaining how he had tossed the robber off the train, and saved their money.

"You ain't from around here, are you?" the deputy asked.

"No, sir, I'm from Boston."

"They grow all of 'em that big in Boston?"

Rob chuckled. "Not everyone."

"Looks like you have a broken nose. If anyone is big enough to break your nose, I sure wouldn't want to run into him," the deputy said with a slight laugh.

Self-consciously, Rob rubbed the bump on his nose with his index finger. "Funny you would say that, because I didn't run into him. He played tackle for Yale, and he ran into me. And I'd just as soon not have him do it again, myself."

The train remained at the depot for about an hour, then once the sheriff and deputy left, it got underway again. Tomorrow, Rob realized, he would leave the train in Flagstaff, Arizona.

CURLY STEVENS HAD WORKED for the Turquoise Ranch for over twenty years, longer than anyone else. Only two others, the ranch foreman, Big Jake Dunford, and the cook, Ed Reynolds, both of whom he had known back in Texas, came close to Curly's longevity. Jake and Ed had been with the ranch only six months less than Curly.

Curly had never seen the real owner of the ranch; no one who worked at the ranch ever had, not even Theodore Matthews who had been the ranch manager when Curly had first arrived, nor Abel Cole, who had been the ranch foreman. Les Garrison, the current ranch manager, and Jake Dunford, the current ranch foreman, were equally ignorant as to who the owner might be. Some said there was no individual owner, that the ranch was held by Morgan, Trevathan, and Daigh. Others said the ranch was just administered by them, and that it was actually owned by English nobility. A few even went so far as to suggest that Queen Victoria was the owner. Because the ranch was owned by an absentee landowner, all authority was in the hands of the ranch manager.

And that, Curly believed, was a problem.

Before Les Garrison had taken the position of ranch manager, he had been a lawyer in Denver. That meant he was a businessman, not a cattleman. Unlike Ted Matthews, who all the men had liked, Garrison was a man with a streak of vanity, and a difficult man to work for. Many of the hands remained only because of their loyalty to Big Jake, who, as the foreman, was second in charge.

Two days earlier, they had received a telegram from Morgan, Trevathan, and Daigh, informing them that a new hand by the name of Rob Barringer would be arriving by train at nine o'clock this evening. There had been some speculation about that; new hands didn't arrive by train, and certainly not with advanced warning by telegram. But the telegram had come, and Big Jake had sent Curly Stevens into town to pick up this new fella.

Curly had brought with him Big Jake's twenty-year-old daughter, Melanie, then dropped her off in front of the hotel, as they would spend the night in town and return to the ranch the next morning. Melanie had come into town so she could take care of some personal business. Melanie's mother, Maggie, had died of meningitis when Melanie was but ten years old, and Big Jake had raised her alone, though he had "Uncle" Curly and "Uncle" Ed to help him.

After Curly put the buckboard away and had the team attended to, he walked back out onto the oardwalk in front of the livery stable. He rubbed his hands together in anticipation of doing a night on the town.

The boardwalk ran the length of the town on both sides of the street. At the end of each block, there were planks laid across the road to allow pedestrians to cross the road without having to walk in the dirt or mud. Curly waited patiently at one of them while he watched a lady cross, holding her skirt up above her ankles daintily, to keep the hem from soiling, then he stepped onto the plank himself. Just as he started to cross the street, he saw Melanie coming back out of the hotel on her way to do her shopping. Curly stepped back and walked in the opposite direction. He had been intending to cross the street and go into the Bull's Hind Quarters, one of the more popular saloons, but he didn't want Melanie to see him. He didn't have to hide his actions from her, as she probably suspected he would visit the saloons anyway. It was just that he didn't want to be quite so blatant about it.

Curly looked in the window of a leather goods shop and contemplated a pair of boots for a moment or two. When he looked back toward Melanie, he saw her stepping into a dry goods store, so he left the window and crossed the street right in the middle of the block, to go into the Bull's Hind Quarters.

It had grown dark enough inside the saloon for the lanterns to be lit, and to accomplish that, a great wagon wheel was lowered from the ceiling by a rope. A bartender held a long match, lighting each of the lanterns which were attached to the wheel.

Curly sidled up to the bar and leaned against it, watching the bartender as he illuminated the fixture. Then he turned back toward the bar to contemplate what he would drink, and he saw his reflection in the mirror behind the bar.

His hair was curly, thus justifying the nickname. But it was no longer jet black. Now it was laced with so much gray that one of his friends had teased him, suggesting that a more suitable nickname might be "Salt and Pepper."

Curly was a relatively short man, though the shortness came from the bowed legs, because his upper body was long. His nose had been broken in a barroom fight which would have been long forgotten had it not been for the constant reminder of it every time he looked at himself in a mirror. He was once a very good barroom fighter and, in his youth, sometimes looked for fights just for entertainment. But he was well into his forties now, and such amusements were no longer as entertaining as they once had been.

He was also exceptionally good with a gun, and was often solicited to be a temporary deputy when the need arose. Twice while acting as a deputy, he had faced off against an outlaw who had entered the duel with the expectations of shooting down a mere deputy. In both cases Curly had prevailed, and those two former outlaws now occupied graves in Potter's Field.

"What'll it be, cowpoke?" the bartender asked as he came back behind the bar and pulled the rope that drew the wagon wheel lamp fixture back into position above the room.

"Whiskey," Curly replied.

The glass was set before Curly, and he took it, then turned with his back to the bar to survey the room. The evening crowd was just beginning to gather. There were several round tables which were full of drinking, laughing customers, and a few where card games were in progress. As Curly watched, one of the players left one of the games, and Curly walked over to the table.

"May I sit in?" he asked.

"Be my guest," a tall man with a handlebar mustache invited.

ROB BARRINGER HAD BEEN on the train for ten days now, and except for the incident when the train was robbed, it had been a trip which was more relaxing, than exhausting, despite the number of days he had been underway. He chuckled quietly as he thought the term, 'underway'. That was a nautical term, one that Rob was quite familiar with, as he had, before getting his degree in law, sailed as a junior officer on one of his grandfather's ships.

He was enjoying watching the changing scenery outside his seat window, and had followed such changing scenery from the congestion and industrialization of the northeast, to the farms and small communities of the Midwest, until the wide-open spaces, desert land, and mountains of the far west.

For this last day, he had particularly enjoyed the mountains, and was looking at one range when a porter walked by his seat.

"Do you know the name of those mountains there?"

"Yes sir, those mountains are the San Francisco Mountains. They're real pretty, ain't they?"

"They are indeed," Rob said. "How much longer until we reach Flagstaff?"

"Oh, I'd say not more'n an hour now."

"Thank, you. You have a good job, don't you? Traveling like you do?"

A wide smile spread across the porter's black face. "I wouldn't trade this job for any other job in the whole country."

"I don't blame you."

"You'll be gettin' off in Flagstaff?" the porter asked.

"Yes."

"Well, I hope you enjoy your stay, sir." The porter

touched his finger to his eyebrow in the form of a salute, then passed on through the car.

WHEN CURLY LEFT the saloon a little over an hour later it was dark and he was broke. He had had very little money to start with, and any hopes of running it up into enough to have a pleasant night on the town were quickly dispelled by his run of bad luck. In truth, Curly didn't actually believe it was all bad luck. He was convinced that the man with the handlebar mustache and another man were working in cahoots to cheat him, though he had no way of proving it. Making an unsubstantiated accusation of cheating could be a dangerous move, and Curly had come into town unarmed. So he bore his losses stoically, though he wished now that he hadn't brought Melanie into town. If it weren't for Melanie, he could just pick up the new hand and head back to the ranch tonight. Now, he would have to wait until morning. All night long in town, and no money to spend. And to make matters worse, he hadn't yet eaten.

Curly thought of the new hand he was to meet. Perhaps he could get him to play a couple of games of two-handed poker on the come. After all, they would be working together; surely the new man would trust his credit. Then Curly stopped. He realized that, if this man was like those who had come before him, he would not likely have any extra money.

He wondered where this new hand would be coming from, and how he had wound up working at Turquoise. Les Garrison was a difficult man to work for, and, as a result, he had a hard time keeping enough hands on to do the work. By now his reputation had spread so that local cowboys didn't want to work for him, so Curly had to believe that this new hand, whose name was Rob Barringer, wouldn't know anything about Garrison.

Curly had stayed on, and so had half a dozen or more of the other, older hands. But they had stayed on, not out of loyalty to Les Garrison, but to the foreman, Big Jake. As a result, he had no interest in leaving now, despite the difficult personality of Les Garrison.

The younger hands had no such loyalty though, so there was a rather rapid turnover, and Curly had seen many new hands come and go. Often, they were green young men, frequently from the East, coming West out of a spirit of adventure. Others were discharged soldiers, interested in trying their hand at cowboying. Some, Curly suspected, were on the dodge from the law and looking for a place to hide out. But they almost always had one thing in common. They were almost always broke, having spent their last cent just to get here. That meant there would be no sense in trying to interest the newcomer in a game of cards. He would, no doubt, be just as broke as Curly was, or else he had spent all his money on a train ticket.

Curly wandered down to the depot to wait for the night train. The depot was one of the most substantial structures in town. It was fairly large, with a waiting room, warehouse, dining room, freight and dispatch offices all inside one building. It was painted green, with a red-painted shake roof and a proud white sign announcing "Flagstaff."

The arrival of the train was always an important event in a small Western town, and Flagstaff was no exception. There was a carnival atmosphere to the crowd. There was a great deal of laughing and joking going on, and a constant cry of salesmen who were trying to take advantage of the crowd to move their wares.

Curly leaned back against the depot wall and watched the crowd mill about on the platform. He rolled a cigarette, lit it, then smoked quietly as he waited for the train.

"Here it comes!" someone shouted, and with the shout, the laughing and joking ceased as everyone grew quiet to await the train's arrival.

Curly watched as the people on the platform moved closer to the track to stare in the direction from which the train would come. Those who looked could see the headlamp first, a huge, wavering yellow disc—actually a gas flame and mirror reflector—shining brightly in the distance. They could hear it now as well, the hollow sounds of the puffing steam came not only from the train, but rolled back in echo from the surrounding mountainsides. As the train grew even closer one could see glowing sparks spewing out from the smokestack, whipped up by the billowing clouds of smoke.

The train pounded into the station with sparks flying from the drive wheels and glowing hot embers dripping from its firebox. Following the engine and tender, were the golden patches of light that were the windows of the passenger cars. Inside, Curly could see that those people who would be getting off here, were already moving toward the exits at the end of the cars.

ROB STEPPED DOWN onto the platform as soon as the train stopped, and stood there, for just a moment, bathed in the escaping steam from the engine. It was quite chilly, and he was surprised at how cool it was.

He had no way of knowing who would be meeting him, and to be honest, wasn't one hundred percent sure anyone would. He decided that if someone was there, the best thing to do would be just to stand there until all the other passengers had left, so that he would be the only one remaining. That way, whoever his contact was would come to him.

CURLY WAS in no hurry to meet the new hand, so he stood quietly until everyone was off the train. Many of the passengers were being met, but there were several who weren't. Most of those who weren't being met were drummers, calling on Flagstaff as part of their circuit. They were easy to pick out, for they were all dressed in business suits, vests and ties, proud emblems of their profession.

The passengers who would be leaving with the train got on, and with the conductor's shout of "All aboard!" a gush of steam and a quick, impatient whistle, the train started up. Curly watched until it was gone, then, on the nearly deserted platform he saw a single figure standing alone, looking around as if trying to decide what he was about to do. Curly knew, without having to be told, that this was the man he was to meet.

The man was big. Curly guessed that he must stand at least six feet three, and thought he weighed over two hundred pounds, none of it fat. He had big shoulders and long, powerful-looking arms. If he couldn't do anything else, he should certainly be good for any job around the ranch that required brute strength, for Curly could tell by looking that here was a man who was exceptionally strong.

As Curly moved closer to him, he couldn't help but feel an affinity with him, because the man had a nose just like Curly's. It had obviously been broken, and Curly smiled as he wondered how big the other fella had been to be able to do that.

The man wasn't handsome by any stretch of the word, but there was something about him that made Curly think he would probably like him. There seemed to be a sense of humor in his eyes and the suggestion of a laugh around his mouth. Curly walked over to him.

"Hello," the big man said, sticking a large mitt out for a friendly handshake. "Are you from the Turquoise Ranch?"

"Yes," Curly said. "Folks call me Curly."

"I'm Rob," the big man said. "Robert Barringer."

Curly laughed.

"What is it? What's wrong?"

"Nothing, really," Curly said. "It's just that out here, we don't often hear a man's full handle."

"Should I not give it?" Rob asked innocently.

"You ain't wanted by the law, are you?" Curly asked.

"No, no, of course not," Rob said easily. "Why would you ask that?"

"If you ain't wanted by the law, there ain't no reason why you can't tell a feller your whole handle iffen you want to," Curly said. "Fac' is—" Curly looked around, then in a quieter voice, he continued sheepishly, "My real name is Joshua. Joshua Stevens. Only, don't many people know that. I prefer to go by Curly."

Rob laughed. "All right, then Curly it shall be," he said. Rob walked over to the baggage cart then, and he picked up a trunk which two men were struggling with and lifted it easily to his shoulder.

"Did you bring a wagon or something into town?"

Rob asked. "I can put away my trunk. Then, if you don't mind, we could go get something to eat. I'm starved."

"I, uh, brought a buckboard," Curly said. "It's over in the livery, about a block from here. That's pretty far to have to carry that. If you want, you can leave it here and I'll go hook up the buckboard."

"No, there's no need," Rob said easily. "Just show me where it is."

Curly led the way down the street toward the livery, and Rob kept up an easy conversation for the entire distance, showing absolutely no strain from carrying the trunk. When they reached the livery, Curly showed Rob the buckboard, and Rob set his load down easily. The buckboard sagged under the weight.

"Now," Rob said, brushing his hands together. "What do you say we get something to eat?"

"I have some jerky here in the buckboard," Curly offered.

"Jerky? Jerky is all right when you have to eat it," Rob said. "But I was thinking more along the lines of a big steak, with a healthy side of potatoes. A half-dozen biscuits would go well with it, too."

"A meal like that would cost nearly a dollar," Curly said. "I don't have any money."

Rob smiled. "Well, I have a little," he said. "In fact, I have enough for both of us. Have you eaten?"

"No," Curly said. He smiled sheepishly. "Truth is, I lost all my money playin' poker to a couple of slick-dealin' galoots a'fore I come down to meet you."

"You don't say? Well, you'll have to show me the fellows you were playing with. I'll want to be sure and avoid them if I get into any poker games."

"Yeah," Curly said grimly. "Yeah, I'd say that would be a pretty good idea."

A SHORT WHILE LATER, Curly pushed his plate away. He was so stuffed that he could scarcely breathe.

"How about passing the rest of the biscuits this way if you aren't going to eat any more of them," Rob asked, and Curly, amazed at Rob's appetite, handed the plate of biscuits across to the big man. Rob had already finished his steak and potatoes, and now he set to work finishing the rest of the biscuits. He had just finished the last one when a couple of men came in through the front door. Curly glanced over toward them and saw that they were the two men in the game he had suspected of cheating. The fact that they were together now, talking and joking, proved that they weren't casual acquaintances who happened to meet in the game. That also tended to substantiate Curly's suspicions.

"Well," Curly said, "there they are."

"Who?" Rob asked.

"Them two men I told you I lost my money to in a poker game."

Rob looked over toward them. One was tall and wore a handlebar mustache. The other was shorter and clean shaven. Both wore city-style clothes.

They sat at a table next to Curly and Rob.

They were laughing, and one of them said something that was so quiet no one else could hear. Both of them laughed again. Their laughter was low and evil, and Curly intuitively knew that it was not the light banter of the kind he was used to with cowboys.

"What did that fella say her name was again?" the tall one asked.

"Melanie," the other answered.

"That's a pretty name, ain't it? Melanie."

"Sure it is," the short one replied. "But then, all whores have got pretty names." He rubbed his crotch and laughed. "Wouldn't I like to crawl in a sleepin' roll with her, though?" he said, and he laughed again, more raucously than before.

Curly tensed, and Rob noticed it.

"What is it?" Rob asked.

"Melanie," Curly said. "They are talkin' about Melanie."

"Who is Melanie?"

"She's the sweetest girl you'd ever want to meet," Curly said. "She's the daughter of our foreman. I brung her into town with me today, and she'll be goin' back with us tomorrow."

"If you are goin' to get in that girl's sleepin' roll, you probably got to wait 'n line. A whore that's a looker like that has probably got a lot of customers," one of the two men said.

"Mister, you mind your tongue!" Curly said. "I'll not listen to that kind of language about Miss Dunford."

"Miss Dunford, is it?" the tall one with the handlebar mustache said. He chuckled. "And who are you, her flunkie?"

"I happen to work at the Turquoise Ranch," Curly said. "And you are spreading filthy lies about a fine young girl."

The shorter of the two men said, "Hey, Luke, you know who this is? This here is the sucker cowboy we took in the poker game. Only he was such shortchange that he wasn't hardly worth the effort."

"Looks like we ain't the only one to take him," Luke replied. "Seems to me like he's been took by the girl as well. What's an old geezer like you doin' sniffin' aroun' a young girl, anyway? Why, she could throw you offen her like a..."

The gambler didn't get a chance to finish his remark, because Curly was over to his table in a flash, and he brought the back of his hand across the gambler's face so hard that it sounded like someone clapping hands.

"Why you dried-up old prairie dog, you hit me!" the gambler said in surprise, running his fingers across his cheek, which was now showing a red welt.

"You're damned right I hit you, and I'm about to do it again if you don't apologize for those remarks about Miss Dunford." Curly drew his hand back again, but he just let it hang there when he saw the gambler draw a small derringer from his jacket pocket.

"No, I don't think you will," the tall gambler said menacingly. "Because I'm going to put a ball right between your eyes." The gambler raised his pistol to fire, but before he could, Rob reached up and clamped his big hand around the gambler's wrist. Rob squeezed the wrist so hard that the gambler let out a yelp of pain, and the gun clattered to the floor.

"Let go of his wrist, mister, or I'll put a bullet in your brain!" the smaller gambler said, and now he was also armed. But he was too preoccupied with keeping a wary eye on Rob to notice Curly, and Curly took advantage of that preoccupation to pick up a chair. He brought it crashing down on the second gambler, who fell like a sack of potatoes. Rob increased the pressure on his man's wrist until the tall man sank to his knees, crying out in pain. Finally Rob released him.

"You damn fool... I think you broke my arm!" the gambler said.

"No," Rob said. "But if I had wanted to do it, I could have done so quite easily."

The gambler was still whimpering in pain and he took off his jacket to look at his arm. When he did, the action revealed a clamp and an accordion-like device on his arm.

"What the...? What is that?" Curly asked.

"It's called a sleeve holdout," Rob said.

"A what?"

Rob reached down and took the device from the gambler's arm.

"It would appear that your suspicions were well-founded," Rob said. "This man was cheating, and this is the proof. It's a small machine, arranged to allow him to slip a card into the palm of his hand anytime he needs it. I once saw a demonstration of just such a device."

"Mister, you owe me two dollars and fifty cents," Curly said.

Slowly, painfully, the gambler reached into his vest pocket and pulled out a handful of money. He dropped it on the table.

"Here," he said. "Take it. Take it all. Just, for God's sake, get this giant away from me!"

"I only want what's mine," Curly said, picking up his share of the money. He put it in his pocket, and looked at the other gambler, who was just beginning to come around. "I think you and your friend should stay out of our sight for the rest of the time we're in town."

"Don't you worry none about that," the gambler said as he helped the other man to his feet. "If I ever see either one of you again, it will be too soon for me."

Both gamblers hurried out of the restaurant while Rob gallantly set the chair back up and carefully moved the tables back to the way they were. He looked at the proprietor of the restaurant, who, when the trouble began, had moved with the other customers to the far side of the room.

"I'm sorry for the disturbance," Rob said. "I hope you will forgive us."

"Mister, those two hyenas have been nothing but trouble ever since they came into town," the restaurant owner said. "Believe me, it does my heart good to see them run off. You don't have my forgiveness. You have my thanks."

"Come on," Curly said, now grinning broadly. "Seein' as how I've got my poke back, I can show you how to have a little fun in this town."

ROB HAD READ about saloons in the dime-novels that had given birth to the interest he had in the West, so he was looking forward to the visit. Almost the moment he and Curly stepped inside, they were met by an attractive young woman who was more scantily dressed than any woman he had ever seen before.

"Oh, honey, you are a big one, aren't you?" she said as she lay her fingers on his cheek.

"He ain't for you, Millie," Curly said. "He ain't quite broke in yet, he's still got too much Eastern in 'im."

"You callin' 'im a tenderfoot are you, Curly?" one of the other saloon customers asked.

Curly smiled, and shook his head. "I ain't callin' him nothin' that he don't want to be called. I've done seen how strong he is."

"Yeah, lookin' at 'im, I'd say that's prob'ly a pretty good idea."

Rob nursed one beer, and was amazed at Curly's capacity for alcohol.

It was after eleven o'clock by the time they left the saloon, and Curly was more than a little unsteady on his feet.

"I hope it isn't too late for us to get a hotel room," Rob said.

"Ha, there ain't no need of us spendin' money on a hotel room, I've got a place for us to stay."

"Oh, good, then you've already got a room."

Curly chuckled. "Yeah, you could say that."

6

When Rob opened his eyes the next morning, he was so cold that he found himself groping for cover. But there was no cover because he wasn't sleeping in a bed; he was sleeping in a stall in the livery stable. For just a moment he wondered where he was, and how he got here. Then he looked over and saw Curly, who was skillfully burrowed down in the straw, sleeping comfortably. When he saw that, he smiled, and he remembered.

Rob made the offer to put them both up in a hotel last night, but Curly wouldn't hear of it. Curly had insisted that Rob save his money. Besides, Curly explained, sleeping in a livery stable was better anyway, because a fella wouldn't feel "cooped up" that way.

That was all well and good for Curly, Rob thought. He had experience in sleeping this way, and he was able to make himself quite comfortable. But Rob had not passed as good a night. It took him a long time to get to sleep, and when he did get to sleep his body was still cold. Now, in the gray light of early morning, he felt exceptionally cold, so he looked around to try and find some way to get warm.

Rob blew on his hands and wrapped his arms around himself, then he saw a saddle blanket hanging across a partition. He smiled as he thought of his grandmother and her insistence that the bed linen be changed every day. What would she think about wrapping up in a saddle blanket, just to get warm? The truth is, Rob didn't relish using it, but it would be better than nothing. In fact, at the moment, Rob was grateful for it. He took the blanket from the partition and wrapped it around his shoulders. The blanket was covered with frost, stiff and cold, but he knew that his body heat would warm it, then it would be better, so he braved the initial discomfort.

There was a window open at the back of the stable, and Rob, holding the blanket securely around his shoulders, went to the window to look outside. From here he could look up to the top of San Francisco Peak, and he could see snow there. Being able to see the snow made him feel all the colder and he saw that it was cool enough to see his breath when he exhaled. That surprised him a little. He had not expected it to be this cool in the mornings this late in the spring. Especially as he had always regarded Arizona as being in a warm climate.

"Well, Grandfather, I am here," Rob said under his breath. "You've spoken of the days when you used to be a stable boy. Was it a stable just like this, I wonder? Well, I just spent the night in this one, so we have come full circle." Rob shivered and wrapped the frosty blanket more tightly around him. "Why didn't you ever tell me it would be so cold, though?"

"O-oh," Curly moaned from the straw in the corner, and Rob was embarrassed that he might have been overheard talking to himself, so he turned and looked in

Curly's direction. Curly was just now sitting up. He rubbed his head gingerly. Straw hung from his hair and clung to his shirt. Rob laughed.

"Good morning," Rob said. "Did you pass a pleasant night?"

Curly looked toward him. His eyelids drooped heavily, and he blinked several times, as if gingerly testing the world he had so reluctantly abandoned the night before.

"Say," Curly said, "by chance, did a horse happen to step on my head during the night?" He rubbed his head again.

"No, my friend," Rob said. "Any pounding in your head comes from within, I'm afraid. You put away a prodigious amount of whiskey last night."

"What did I do?" Curly asked, not understanding the comment.

"You drank a lot," Rob said simply.

Curly smiled. "Did I have a good time?"

"You appeared to have a wonderful time," Rob said.

Curly stood up, then walked over to a watering trough. He bent over and stuck his head down in it, then jerked it out again, shaking the cold water from his face and hair and making a *brrring* sound with his lips. Rob winced because he couldn't bear to think of immersing his head in cold water on a morning as cold as this.

"I *hope* I had a good time," Curly said. He began combing out his hair with his fingers. "I hope it was worth all this."

"Well, what do you say?" Rob asked. "Are you about ready for breakfast?"

"Breakfast?" Curly moaned. He shook his head. "No, thank you. I don't think I could look food in the face this morning."

"Come on," Rob said. "A half-dozen eggs or so, a few

pieces of ham and a handful of biscuits would fix you right up."

Curly looked pale. "If you mention food again, tenderfoot, I'll shoot you where you stand," he said menacingly.

"How are you going to shoot me? You don't have a gun," Rob teased.

"Damned if I don't," Curly agreed. "Then I'll strangle you with my bare hands, and..." Curly started, then, looking at Rob and his size, he stopped in mid-sentence and groaned. "Oh, please, can't you just have mercy on me?"

"All right." Rob laughed. "I won't insist that you eat breakfast. But I hope you don't mind if I do."

"No, I don't mind," Curly said. "Only be back here right after, 'cause as soon as Miss Melanie is ready, we'll be headin' back to the ranch."

"I'll be here," Rob promised.

Rob stripped off his shirt and washed himself at the water trough, braving the cold water in the name of cleanliness. After he washed, he opened his suitcase, then he pulled out a clean, light-blue shirt and put it on. Curly watched him.

"What'd you do?" Curly asked. "Roll over inter somethin' while you was asleep? The stable keep said this was a clean stall."

"No, I didn't roll into anything," Rob said as he buttoned the shirt.

"Then what are you puttin' on another shirt for?" he asked.

"I just felt the need for one," Rob answered without elaboration. "Don't you ever feel like just changing shirts?"

"I only got me three," Curly said. "An' one of them is

my Sunday go-to-meetin' shirt, only since I don't go to Sunday meetin's, I don't hardly never wear it none. The other two shirts I wear one week at a time, then I change."

"This is my week," Rob said.

"Oh," Curly replied, and that seemed to satisfy him. "Don't forget now, you come back here right after breakfast. I don't want to keep Miss Melanie waitin' on account a some tenderfoot that can eat more'n any three men I ever knowed."

"All right," Rob answered.

Rob left the livery stable and walked along the boardwalk. He looked around the town, seeing it in daylight for the first time. In the bright light of day, the town didn't seem quite as intimidating. It wasn't nearly as large as he had imagined it to be last night. And it wasn't nearly as boisterous either.

Last night Rob had seen Flagstaff only by the golden glow of the many lamps and lanterns which splashed patches of light onto the streets. With Curly, he had started on one side of the street, gone into every saloon they encountered, then they crossed the street and went into every one on the other side as they worked their way back.

Rob had enjoyed it, even though he did no more than nurse a beer in each of the saloons. He enjoyed it because it was all new and strange to him, and he was absorbing new experiences. He watched the bargirls and the gamblers and the cowboys with an intense, though guarded interest. Guarded, because he did not want to make anyone uneasy by this observation.

Curly drank straight whiskey as if that were his mission in life. The bargirls fluttered to them like moths to a light as soon as the men stepped through the swinging doors of a new saloon. They were drawn to Rob by his size, and to Curly by the hope that he would be generous enough to spread some of his money around. When they discovered that Rob wasn't interested in anything they had for sale and that Curly was doing a maximum amount of drinking on a minimum investment, the girls left them alone, and Curly, after finishing a drink in one bar, would leave abruptly and head for another. By the time they left the final saloon, Curly was staggering drunk, and Rob had to help him back to the livery stable.

Rob planned to take his breakfast at the restaurant where he and Curly had eaten dinner last night, but as he passed the hotel, he saw that it also had a restaurant. Since it was close to the livery stable, and since he had promised Curly he would return immediately, he thought it would be more convenient to eat his breakfast here. He stepped inside and went to the dining room.

———

MELANIE WAS in the hotel dining room, looking at the menu, trying to decide what to order for breakfast. A shadow fell across her table, and it was so large that it seemed as if the very sun had been blotted out. She looked up to see a tall man standing in the door looking around the dining room. He wasn't just tall, he was very big, with wide shoulders and long, powerful-looking arms. The man looked over the dining room for a moment, saw an empty table, then walked over to it. Melanie watched him as he moved. Despite his great size he moved with a fluid gracefulness which was pleasant to watch. Melanie was reminded of a powerful stallion with a sleek black coat and muscles which rippled just under the skin.

Melanie's father was a big man, hence the name Big Jake. And because of her father, as a little girl she had always thought that she would grow up to marry a big man. How different things were about to turn out, for Les, the man she was engaged to, was considerably smaller than her father. This man, on the other hand, was even bigger than her father.

Melanie continued to stare at him as he took his seat. She covered her curiosity by holding the menu in front of her face. The man's eyes, she couldn't help noticing, were light blue. In fact, their color very nearly matched his shirt. He looked up as the waiter brought him a menu, and he smiled an easy, comfortable smile. The smile did something to his face. It softened the rough features and minimized the effect of the misshapen nose.

Melanie ate a light breakfast, not because she wasn't hungry, but because she wanted to leave the dining room as quickly as she could. When she did leave a few moments later, she managed to steal one more glance at the tall man. She was relieved to see that he was now occupied with his own breakfast. Because of that, she was able to get away without another awkward glance.

"Oh, Miss Dunford," Eb Deckert called out as Melanie walked through the lobby. "What do you want me to do with these things you bought yesterday?"

"Curly will be by for me shortly," Melanie said. "Just have them stacked up out front, and Curly will pick them up in the buckboard."

"Yes, ma'am, I will," Eb said. "Oh, and Miss Dunford, you won't be too hard on Curly, will you? After all, it was you he was fighting over."

Melanie had just started up the stairs to her room,

but when she heard that, she stopped and looked over toward the front desk in confusion.

"What?" she asked. "What are you talking about? Who fought over me?"

"Why, Curly did," Eb said. "That is, Curly and the new hand he picked up. They took on those two tinhorn gamblers that have been robbin' ever'one in town. The robbers both had guns, and Curly and your new man were unarmed, but that didn't stop 'em." Eb chuckled. "No, ma'am, that didn't slow 'em down one whit. And after they was through, why them two no-'count gamblers lit out. Truth to tell, I think they even left town."

"Why they were fighting over me?" Melanie asked.

Eb blinked a couple of times, then cleared his throat, realizing that he may have spoken out of turn.

"Uh, well, nothin' much," he said.

"Mr. Deckert, if Curly fought over me, there must have been something."

"I… I think the two tinhorns passed some uncomplimentary remark about you, that's all," Eb said.

"But, how can that be? I don't even know the two men you're talking about."

"The thing is, I think they seen you yesterday when you was shoppin'," Eb said. "You know how men like that are sometimes. They can be awful insultin', just from meanness."

"I see," Melanie said, "and over some stupid remark they may have made, Curly felt it was necessary to defend my honor, is that it?"

"Yes, Miss Melanie, I reckon it was," Eb said. "'Course, it wa'nt only Curly. It was the new hand, too. They was together."

"Thank you for the information," Melanie said.

"Yes," Eb said. "Well, uh, I only tole you this 'cause you might of heard it somewhere else, 'n they might not have got all the facts straight. It wa'nt Curly's fault, Miss Melanie."

"Oh, I'm sure it wasn't," Melanie said coolly. "And you are right, Mr. Deckert, I'm glad I heard it from you first."

7

A few moments later Melanie was standing on the front porch of the hotel, patting her foot impatiently as she waited for Curly to show up with the buckboard. Her purchases were in boxes, stacked neatly beside her. She had bought material, ribbons, and lace for a dress to wear at her wedding party. Mrs. Ivery, the seamstress, had come to the valley with her husband about a year ago. Mr. Ivery was a lumberjack, and he had a contract to cut lumber from the Turquoise Ranch. For the year or so it would require to take the lumber out, the Iverys were living in one of the range cabins on the ranch, so it would be very convenient for her to make the dress.

The buckboard arrived shortly after Melanie came out onto the porch, and Curly pulled it up to the porch and stopped it, then hopped down to start loading the packages. He helped Melanie onto the seat.

"I thought you picked up a new hand last night," Melanie said.

"I did," Curly said. "He's back at the stable, takin' care of the bill. We'll go back and pick him up."

Melanie was tempted to take Curly to task now for his unauthorized defense of her honor on the night before, but if the new hand had been involved, she decided she might as well wait and include him. After all, if she let them know right now how she felt about such things, perhaps it would prevent it from ever happening again.

Curly swung the team in a wide, U-turn in the street in front of the hotel and drove back over to the livery stable. He stopped out front and gave a loud whistle.

"Ah, there he is," Curly said and chuckled under his breath. "Oh, I forgot to tell you. He's a big 'un."

Rob came out of the barn and started to get onto the buckboard.

"You!" Melanie said, mouthing the word with such expressiveness that both Rob and Curly looked at her in surprise.

"Miss Melanie, do you... do you know Rob?" Curly asked.

"No, I don't know him," Melanie went on. "But I'm angry with him. And you, too! Curly, just what makes you think I could possibly appreciate your fighting, for whatever reason?" she asked. "And to bring me into it..."

"Now, hold on, Miss Melanie. I didn't bring you into it, those two galoots did," Curly said. "Miss Melanie, you don't know what all they was a' sayin'."

"You should have just let them babble on," Melanie said. "What did it matter what they were saying? It is obviously untrue."

"But Miss Melanie, it was a matter of honor," Curly protested.

"Is it honorable to bring me into a... a common saloon fight?"

"It wasn't a saloon, it was a restaurant," Curly said.

"Then all the more reason you should have done nothing. If you were offended by what they were saying, there were other things you could have done, other ways you could have fought."

"Like what?" Curly asked.

"Well, you could have ignored them," Melanie suggested.

"What? And do nothing?" Curly asked.

"Yes."

"But... what good would that have done?" Curly asked.

"I think what Miss Dunford is suggesting, is that discretion is the better part of valor," Rob said.

Melanie looked around in quick surprise.

"Something like that, yes," she said. "Though I wouldn't have expected to hear such a remark from you."

"Why would you say that? Is it because you think that a man of my size is given to unruly behavior?"

"No, not that. It is your choice of words that surprised me."

Rob chuckled. "I see. Well, admittedly Shakespeare's version in the play Henry IV actually reads, 'Valor is the better part of discretion,' but the line is most frequently spoken as I did."

"You... you've read Shakespeare? You went to school?"

"Yes."

"I wouldn't have thought..." Melanie let the sentence die.

"You wouldn't think a big, dumb-looking brute like me would go to school, is that it?"

"I didn't say that," Melanie replied quickly.

"You didn't have to," Rob said. "I know what people think about men my size. They think we are all dumb."

"Your size has nothing to do with it at all," Melanie said. "I was thinking more along the lines of the profession you've chosen for yourself. You are obviously an educated man. Why would an educated man want to be a cowboy?"

"A spirit of adventure?" Rob replied.

"Well, I beg of you, Rob, don't get your adventure by defending my honor. My honor doesn't need defending."

Melanie called him Rob, because she called all the hands by their first names. And yet, for some reason, she felt self-conscious about doing it with him.

WHEN CURLY STOPPED in front of the foreman's house, Jake came out to meet them.

"Hello, Papa," Melanie said, kissing him on the cheek.

"Everything go all right in town?" Jake asked.

"It went fine," Melanie said.

"Jake, this here giant calls hisself Rob Barringer," Curly said. "Rob, this is Jake Dunford, the foreman. I've knowed 'im for a long time, 'n he's as fine a man as I've ever knowed."

"It's good to meet you, Mr. Dunford," Rob said, extending his hand.

"It's good to have you joining us," Jake replied, taking the hand.

"I'd better warn Ed about him," Curly said.

"Warn Ed?" Jake asked.

Curly chuckled. "Yeah, I've seen this feller eat. Ed's goin' to have to order in more food."

"I take it Ed is the cook?" Rob said.

"Best belly-robber in Arizona. He's been here a long time, too. He cooked for the cap'n during the war."

"The captain?"

"That would be me," Jake said with an acknowledging smile. "I was a Captain for the Confederacy during the unpleasantness."

"Papa, I got a new pouch of tobacco for Les while I was in town. I'm going to take it over to him," Melanie said.

"You do that," Jake said. "Rob, why don't you come in and have a cup of coffee with me so we can get to know each other better?"

"Yes, sir, that sounds like a good idea," Rob said, and as Curly drove off to put the buckboard away, and Melanie started toward the Big House, Rob followed Jake inside.

"How long have you been foreman here?" Rob asked, as Jake handed him a cup of coffee.

Jake chuckled. "Young man, that's not the way it works. I'm the foreman and you're the new hand. That means I ask you first."

Rob laughed as well. "You're right, of course. Forgive me, my indiscretion was brought on by my anxiousness to become part of the fabric of Turquoise Ranch."

"Indiscretion," Jake said. "Well, young man, that gives me an opening for our discussion. One of the questions I normally ask a new hand is whether or not he can read and write. It's rather obvious that I don't need to ask you such a thing. How is it that you have such a vocabulary? How far did you go in school?"

"I have a bachelor's degree in business from Harvard," Rob said, easily. He said nothing of his *juris doctor* in law, because he thought it better to keep that to himself.

Jake wouldn't have been more shocked if Rob had slapped him in the face.

"You have a college degree in business?"

"Yes, sir. That's where I got this." Rob smiled as he held his hand to his nose. "I ran into a Yale lineman in our twenty-eight to zero loss."

"Rob, you'll excuse me for asking, but just why in the hell would someone with a college degree be willing to work on a ranch?"

"Would you believe it's for the adventure?"

"Don't tell me. You've been reading dime novels."

Rob chuckled. "I know they will never be classified as literature, but yes, I've read, and enjoyed them. And yes, even though I know they are novels, and exaggerated, as most novels are, they are what gave me a thirst to come West for adventure."

"Well, I don't think you will find any 'dime-novel' type adventure here," Jake said. "At least, I certainly hope not."

8

"It's good to see you back," Garrison said, kissing Melanie lightly on the cheek. "Did you have any problem finding everything you wanted in town?"

"No," Melanie said, "everything went just fine."

"Who is the big, dumb lummox you and Curly brought back with you?"

"Don't let his size fool you," Melanie said. "He isn't dumb," she added with conviction.

"Oh?" Les replied, raising an eyebrow as he spoke. "How did you find out so quickly? What did he do, recite poetry for you or something?"

Melanie chuckled. "In a matter of speaking he did, I suppose. He quoted Shakespeare. I get the feeling he isn't dumb."

"Then what's he doing working for twenty-one dollars a month and found?" Les challenged.

"I don't know," Melanie admitted. "He told me he's looking for adventure."

"He must talk a great deal. Either that, or perhaps you just have a little more than the usual interest in this cowboy. I don't think I like that, and I don't think I'm going to like him very much."

"Oh, don't be silly, Les," Melanie said quickly. "I don't have any more or any less interest in him than in anyone else. He's just another cowboy, that's all."

"That's right," Garrison said. "He's just another cowboy. Where is he now?"

"He's talking to Papa."

"Tell your father to send him over to see me. I'd like to interview this new hand."

"Why would you want to do that? Papa's the foreman, and he's always the one who interviews the new hands."

"Let's just say that I've taken an interest in this smart cowboy."

"All right, I'll send him over."

JAKE WAS LAUGHING at something Rob had said, when Melanie returned to the house.

"Hello, Sweetheart. Did Les appreciate the tobacco?" Jake greeted.

"Yes. Rob, he wants to see you."

"What?" Jake asked. "Why? Since when did the ranch manager start interviewing new hands?"

"I don't know. I just know that he asked me to send Rob over to him."

"It's the Big House," Jake said, pointing. "That's where the owner would live, if he lived here. That is, assuming there is an owner."

"Wait, are you saying nobody owns Turquoise Ranch?" Rob asked.

"Oh, I'm sure that somebody owns it, but I'm beginning to think, after all these years, that it's owned by some corporation, and not any one man."

———————

ROB WALKED over to the Big House, stepped up onto the porch and was about to knock on the door when the door opened.

"You're the new man?"

"Yes."

"Since I am to be your boss, yes sir would be appropriate."

"As Jake Dunford is the foreman of Turquoise Ranch, I assumed that he would be my boss."

"He's the foreman, but I am the ranch manager, which means I am his boss."

"But don't ranch managers typically tend to the business of the ranch, while the foremen deal more with the men, and the day-to-day operation?"

"Let's just say that I am more of a hands-on type of manager. Do you have a problem with that?"

"No problem at all, Mr. Garrison. On the contrary, I would say that is certainly a favorable attribute for a ranch manager."

"Well, I'm glad you approve," Garrison said, his voice dripping with sarcasm. "Step onto the porch with me."

Rob followed him and Les pointed out the bunkhouse. "That's where you will live. See Curly and he'll select a horse for you. He'll also give you the rules of the ranch. But the most important rule of all is that you remember your place around Miss Dunford."

"Remember my place?" Rob replied. "And just what would that place be?"

"You know what that place is," Garrison said. "You

are nothing but a hired hand. In fact, you are the lowest and least important hand on this ranch. I am going to marry Miss Dunford. I don't want you near her, do you understand?"

Rob looked at Les. "Do you give such instructions to every hand on the ranch?"

"No," Les replied. "That isn't necessary."

"Then why do you consider it necessary with me?"

"Because I don't like the way uh... there is no reason, really. It's just a word to the wise, that's all. Now, get your tack put away while I go find Big Jake. I'll see to it that he finds some work for you to do."

Rob returned to the buckboard for his trunk, while Les went over to the foreman's house to speak with Jake.

"I've interviewed the new hand," Les told Jake.

"Yes, I visited with him for a few minutes. He's a big man, who is also very well educated. I find him to be quite an interesting fellow."

"Yes, it does make you wonder why such a man would want to work as a ranch hand. I'm going to take a special interest in him."

AS WITH ALL NEW COWBOYS, the jobs Rob received were the worst of the lot. For the next several days he dug fence-post holes, stretched barbed wire, pitched hay, and greased wagon axles. All were jobs that had to be done, but they were a far cry from the spirit of adventure Rob had hoped for when he came West.

Near the end of the first week, Rob drew the assignment of stringing fence again for the third day in a row. He took a wagonload of wire out to the outer fence line, and there he began to work.

As he worked Rob stripped off his shirt, seeking some relief from the heat. It was a little cooler without his shirt, but he had to be careful, lest he get sunburned.

The wood of the wagon was bleached white by the sun, and it gave off a pungent aroma as it baked in the afternoon heat. Rob picked up a big roll of barbed wire and carried it over to one of the posts he had just put in. He nailed one end of the wire to the post and started stringing the wire out toward the next post. Then he heard someone approaching.

When he looked up, he saw Melanie Dunford. He smiled at her.

Melanie had ridden out to Mrs. Ivery's cabin to bring her the material the seamstress would be using for Melanie's wedding dress. It was such a lovely day for a ride that she decided to take the long way back. That was when she saw Rob Barringer stringing the wire. She saw him before he saw her, and she stopped her horse and stared down at him for a moment. He was working without a shirt, and she could see his smooth muscles flexing under the sun. He reminded her of some animal, a mountain lion, sleek and powerful, and she got the unbidden image of a lion leaping upon its prey. She shuddered, for instinctively she knew that she could easily be his prey. A moment later she found herself approaching him, and he looked up at her and smiled.

"Good morning, Miss Dunford," he said. His voice was deep, well-modulated and cultured, and it would never cease to surprise Melanie to hear such a voice come from such a powerful-looking man.

"Don't you know better than to work out in this sun without some protection?" Melanie asked. "You will burn very badly."

Melanie swung down from her horse and walked

over to him. His shoulders were already red, and she put her fingers on his skin there. When she moved her fingers away, they left little white marks on his skin. Rob winced in pain.

"Do you see what I mean?" she asked.

"Yes," Rob said. He started for his shirt and gave a little self-conscious laugh. "I guess I'm not used to the Arizona sun." He started to put the shirt on, then he winced even more as the rough texture of the shirt material came into contact with his skin.

"Here," she said. "You'd better let me help. I'll hold the shirt and you try and put your arms into the sleeves."

Rob winced as he put the shirt on.

"When you get back, see Ed. I'll have him mix up a concoction of borax and camphor. Put that on your back and it'll work as a sun screen to keep you from burning any worse than you are now."

"All right, thanks, I appreciate that," Rob said.

"Well, I'd better get back. In the meantime, keep your shirt on until you get that sun screen from Ed."

"I will," Rob said with a welcoming grin.

Melanie got back on her horse, then slapping her heels against the side of the horse, she rode away at a gallop.

***

ROB SPENT the next few hours thinking about Melanie's strange visit. He had lots of time to think, for stringing wire was a solitary job, and there was no one there to disturb his thoughts. The work was not only lonely, it was hard. It was backbreaking and often painful, and he had several cuts and punctures from the barbs on the wire. Then, later in the day, Curly happened by. Rob straightened up and wiped his face with his bandana, happy to see the one cowboy who did not treat him like the tenderfoot he was.

"Hi, Curly," Rob called.

"They got you stringin' wire again?" Curly replied. He swung down from his horse and took a long drink of water from his canteen.

"Yep," Rob answered. "By the time I get finished with this wire, I'm going to have the entire territory of Arizona fenced in. No one will be able to come or go," he teased.

Curly put the cap back on his canteen, and wiped his mouth with the back of his hand. A dark stain of perspiration spread from beneath his arms, and Rob wondered in passing when Curly would deem it necessary to put on a new shirt. This was still the same shirt Curly had worn to pick him up, and that was nearly a week ago.

"What I want to know is, which one of the bosses did you go 'n get mad at you?" Curly asked. "Was it the foreman or the manager?"

"Mad at me? Why would one of them be mad at me?"

"That's what I don't know," Curly said. "But you must have done somethin'. Elsewise, they wouldn't keep you on this detail for a whole week. This is punishment kind of work. They don't make nobody, not even a tenderfoot like you, do more'n his share of this kind of work. You must'a made somebody mad."

Curly swung back onto his horse, gave Rob a slight tip of his hat and went back to whatever duties he was attending to that day.

Rob, on the other hand, had to return to his own duties. He worked hard for the remainder of the day, stringing as much wire as any three men could do on an ordinary day. Then, after supper that night he made a special effort to get cleaned up. He intended to go to Big Jake and find out just what was going on. Why was he being singled out for such disagreeable duty?

It wasn't dark yet, though the sun was low in the west, leaving in its wake a brilliant sky splashed with reds and purples. Rob was admiring the view from the front porch of the foreman's house when the door opened. It was Melanie who had answered his knock.

"Hello, Rob, what can I do for you?"

"I would like to speak with Mr. Dunford."

"All right, please, come on in. I'll go get Papa."

Rob walked inside, then stood in the living room with his hat in his hand while Melanie went to get her father. He had been in the house once before, when he first arrived, but he had not really looked around much during that visit. Now he examined the room. There was nothing remarkable about the furnishings; an over-stuffed sofa and chair, a cane-bottom rocking chair, and a lamp table. The kerosene lamp on the table had not yet been lit, but the many glass facets which hung from the mantle shroud shone with the last reflected light of the setting sun. On the wall was a large, oval-framed picture of an attractive woman, and Rob noticed some resemblance between the woman and Melanie. He guessed it must have been Melanie's mother.

"Yes, Rob, did you want to see me?" Jake asked, coming into the room with Melanie at that moment.

"If you don't mind," Rob said politely.

"Papa, I'm going to step over to see Les for a few minutes," Melanie said

"What on earth for?" Jake answered. "You were with him most of the afternoon."

"It's just that Les wanted my help in planning the guest list," Melanie explained.

"All right, but don't stay over there too long, darlin'," Jake advised. "It'll soon be dark, and that won't look too good to the cowboys."

"Papa, Les and I *are* engaged," Melanie said with a pointed look at Rob as if by that statement showing him exactly where things stood. "I'll be moving into the Big House soon."

"You may be engaged, but you aren't married," Jake said. "Don't stay there too long."

"I won't," Melanie promised, kissing her father on the cheek.

Jake watched his daughter leave before he turned back to Rob.

"I wish—" he started. Then, realizing that he was about to think aloud, he cut his remark short. "Never mind. What is it you wanted to see me about?"

"It's about the work you're having me do," Rob said. "Curly says that it isn't routine to assign such tasks to the new men on a permanent basis."

"I see," Jake said. "Is the work too hard for you?"

"No," Rob said. "It isn't that, it's just…"

"It's just not what you had in mind when you came West," Jake finished for him.

"No, this isn't what I had in mind at all."

Jake walked over to the lamp table and picked up a pipe which lay there. He filled the pipe with tobacco from a pouch in his pocket, then he lit the pipe and blew out a long cloud of blue smoke before he spoke again.

"Tell me," Jake said, "exactly what did you have in mind when you came out here?"

"I'm not certain," Rob admitted. "But I didn't think I'd spend all my time stringing fence."

"You admitted to having read some of the dime novels? Did Ned Buntline's action stories get you to thinking that there would be an Indian or a cattle rustler behind every rock?"

"No," Rob said. "Not exactly."

"But you have read the stories?" Jake said.

"Who hasn't?" Rob defended himself.

"I'd say most of the cowboys I've known haven't read them, and for a very good reason. They can't read."

"Oh, I'm sure there must be a few who can't read," Rob said, "but would you go so far as to say most of them can't read?"

"That's right," Jake said. He studied Rob through narrowed eyes. "You take Ed, now. He's the best cook I've ever known, but he's had to teach himself everything. Ed has never read a recipe, nor is he likely to, because he can't read. Neither can your friend, Curly."

"I knew Curly was an uneducated man, but..."

"Hold on there," Jake interrupted. "I didn't say Curly was uneducated. I said he couldn't read. There's a difference between not being able to read and being uneducated. A big difference. In the things Curly does, he has as good an education as any man you might ever run across. He can read trail sign, he can doctor cattle, he can ride a horse like he was a part of the animal. No sir, Curly isn't uneducated. You might even say that he has a doctorate in life."

"I really didn't mean that the way it sounded," Rob apologized. "I suppose it did sound pretentious, didn't it? I apologize."

"Pretentious," Jake scoffed. He took a deep breath. "All right, Rob, your apology is accepted."

"Thanks," Rob answered.

"Tell me, Rob, are you sorry you came out West?"

"No, not at all," Rob replied quickly.

"Even though it isn't what you expected?"

"As I said, I'm not sure what I expected," Rob admitted sheepishly.

"Well, I can tell you this," Jake said. "Despite what you may have read in Mr. Buntline's stories, cowboying isn't adventurous. It's hard work. And don't think ridin' the crooked trail is any more glamorous, because it isn't. You've no idea what it's like to sleep out in the rain or the cold because you're afraid to show your face in town. You don't know what it's like to have paper on you all over the country so that no matter where you go you see your picture staring back at you from a wanted poster The rewards get bigger and bigger until soon you're afraid to sleep, even around your friends."

Rob looked at Jake in some surprise, and for a moment he thought he saw a distant, haunted expression in his eyes. Then Jake cleared his throat and the expression left his face. He smiled.

"I knew a desperado once, and he used to tell me stories," Jake explained. "But, back to the business at hand. Cowboyin' is honest work, but it's hard work."

"Yes, sir, I know," Rob said.

"Digging holes, stringing wire, pitching hay and the like is part of that work," Jake went on.

"I realize that, too," Rob answered.

"What if I told you that I was going to keep you doing that kind of work from now on? Would you quit?"

"No, sir," Rob replied.

"Why not?"

"Because, as you say, it is important. Someone has to do it, and you are the boss. If you think I am better utilized doing that kind of work than I would be doing something else, then that's the kind of work I'll do."

"Without complaint?"

"None, other than the complaint I've just registered,

and as far as I'm concerned, you've explained it to my satisfaction. You may rest assured, that I will make no further protests."

Big Jake puffed on his pipe for a moment longer and just stared at Rob. "What is your relationship to Les Garrison?" Jake finally asked.

"I beg your pardon?"

"Do you know Les Garrison from somewhere?"

"No, I never met him before I came here," Rob replied. "Why do you ask?"

"No reason, I guess," Jake said. "But he took such a special interest in you when you arrived that it makes me wonder a bit. I been thinkin' on the possibility that you might be workin' for him."

Rob laughed. "Of course I'm working for him," he said. "We all are, aren't we?"

"I didn't mean workin' for the ranch, I meant workin' for Les personally," Jake said.

Rob was puzzled by the strange comment, and his expression reflected his bewilderment.

"What do you mean, working for him personally?" Rob asked.

Jake paused for a moment, as if measuring Rob. "You are an intelligent and educated man, Rob, and I must confess that I like what I have seen of you. I should learn to trust my instincts more 'n my suspicions less. Still, there's somethin' strange goin' on around here, and in the long run, I think it pays a fella to be cautious."

"Strange? In what way? Mr. Dunford, what on earth are you talking about?"

"Well, I'll tell you now that it's nothin' you're goin' to have to worry about," Jake said. "But if my suspicions are correct, well, I reckon there's goin' to be some trouble around here. A few heads are goin' to roll when the ranch owners find out what's goin' on. I'm innocent of it 'n that's the God's truth. But like most men, I've got a background that won't stand too much lookin' into. When things start happenin' around here, I'm likely to be the first one to get the blame. And it's probably only right, since I am the foreman and it won't seem likely that anythin' can go on around here without my knowin' of it." Jake took several more long, thoughtful puffs on his pipe. "Maybe I'm a foolish old man, and I'm suspicious for no good reason."

"Mr. Dunford, are you saying the owner of this ranch is being cheated?" Rob asked. Rob obviously had more than a casual interest in the question, though he thought it best to keep the degree of his interest quiet for the time being.

Big Jake dumped the contents of his pipe in a nearby ashtray, then he took out a pocket knife and started cleaning out the bowl. He worked diligently for a long moment before he looked back at Rob.

"All I know is that we are moving more cattle to market than we ever have, but the profit keeps going down. Now how can that be, unless something underhanded is going on?"

"Have you investigated it?"

Jake let out an explosive laugh which had no humor.

"Now why the blazes should I do that? If I'm right, who would I report it to? Garrison? Chances are he's the one doing it, 'n if he's not, then that lays the blame squarely onto me. And if he is doing it, how would I report it to the owners? I don't even know who they are. The truth is, whoever they are, they've probably already forgotten Turquoise Ranch. They're probably so rich that they don't even care what happens out here. I tell you what I should be doing."

"What's that?"

"I should be getting in on this thing, grabbing off as much for myself as I can. Instead, it's all goin' to break someday, and I'm the one that's going to be left holding the bag."

"Maybe not," Rob said. "Maybe the situation is not quite as hopeless as you believe."

"Yeah, it could be you're right," Big Jake said. "And it could be there's nothing at all going on. Still..." Jake let the word hang for a moment. "Well," he finally said, "for Melanie's sake, I sure do hope I'm wrong."

Rob was silent, for it was obvious that a reply wasn't expected. Finally, Jake looked at Rob and smiled.

"Well, but that's neither here nor there for you, is it, young man? You got a itch to be more of a cowboy 'n less of a handyman. I can't say that I blame you any. I apologize for airing my suspicions, and you have my word that things will be different for you from now on. Now, get on back about your business, 'n let me be to mine. Oh, and Rob?"

"Yes?" Rob answered.

"I'd take it kindly if you didn't say anything about our conversation. I was just thinking out loud anyway, and like as not, there's nothing to it. You will keep quiet?"

"Yes, sir," Rob said.

"You're a good man," Jake replied. He chuckled. "You may be nothing but a cowboy now, but I got my suspicions that you've been more in the past, and you'll be more in the future."

Rob was too surprised by Jake's comment to offer a reply. Leaving Big Jake's house, he walked across the yard to the corral. Inside the corral were several horses, and two of them were nibbling playfully on each other's neck. Beyond the corral was the barn, and beyond that, the wide-open spaces which led to Turquoise Peak. Rob was just beginning to realize how beautiful Turquoise Ranch was.

And, he thought with a thrill which sent a small chill shivering through him, he owned it!

9

Melanie stood at the fireplace in the Big House, watching the flames consume a log. The fire popped and snapped, and the flame that licked hungrily at the wood was blue at the base, then it passed through various shades of red, orange and yellow until, at the tip, it curled away into smoke.

Les, who was pleasantly surprised by her unexpected appearance, walked up behind her.

"On a night like this when there is just a bit of a nip outside and a warm fire inside, there is nothing better than a glass of good wine," Garrison said. Melanie heard the tinkle of glasses, then the splashing sound of wine being poured. Les handed her a glass. The deep red liquid glowed brightly in the reflection of the fire, as if it had trapped some inner flame of its own.

"Thank you," Melanie said.

"To us, my dear, and to a future of many evenings as pleasant as this." Les held his glass up and Melanie touched the rim of hers to his. There was a pleasant ring as the glasses touched.

"Drink up, my dear," Garrison said.

Melanie drank the wine and tasted the controlled fire of its fruit on her tongue. When she finished, she held her glass out for a second, and then a third. As the wine began to take effect, she felt a relaxing warmth course through her, and, or so it seemed, that relaxation stilled some of the confusion and turmoil which raged within.

She thought about Rob Barringer, and wondered why he intrigued her so. It couldn't be because of his handsome features, for, compared to Les, Rob wasn't handsome at all. Melanie looked at Les. She had to admit that Les Garrison was an exceptionally handsome man. His features were well-formed, almost aristocratic, and his eyes were penetrating and his lips were full and sensual.

Les sensed that Melanie was staring at him, and he smiled.

"Is something wrong?" he asked.

"No," Melanie said. "Nothing is wrong. I was just thinking what a handsome man you are, that's all."

"Careful, Melanie," Garrison said. "It can be dangerous for a woman to tell a man she thinks he's handsome."

"Why?" Melanie asked innocently.

"I think you know why," Garrison said. "My God, you are a beautiful woman," He put his hand on the bare skin of her neck, and the implied intimacy made her nervous.

"Les, please!" she said. "I must be going now."

"Melanie, we are engaged. Soon you will be my wife."

"I know, but I ask you please, to just be patient."

AFTER ROB LEFT the foreman's house, but before Melanie returned, Jake went over to the fireplace and sat down to watch the flames lick at the wood. He knew that Melanie was visiting with Les right now, and he was somewhat worried about that.

Because her mother had died when she was only ten years old, Jake had raised Melanie without a woman's influence. Melanie had grown into a fine young woman, and Jake wanted only that she be happy. But he couldn't help but wonder if Les was the best person to make her happy.

There were times, since Maggie had died, that Jake had considered marrying again. Not because he found a woman that he thought he could love, but because he thought it would be good to have a woman to help him raise Melanie.

The more he thought of it, though, the more he realized how unfair it would be to the woman he married. And now that Melanie was a fully grown woman, it was too late—her character and personality were fully formed. And to be honest, Jake realized that Melanie was a fine woman, with consideration for others.

Melanie was also a very intelligent young woman, and though Jake was somewhat concerned about her growing relationship with Les, he realized that he should just trust that she would do the right thing.

THE NEXT MORNING Rob was shaken awake while it was still dark.

"Hey, Rob Tenderfoot, roll out of that sack," Curly said. "You been wantin' some real cowboyin', well, it starts now. Get up 'n see how you like it."

Curly was cheerful enough, but at this early hour and

this stage of sleepiness, Rob could have done with a little less cheer and a little more sensitivity.

Rob sat up and felt the chill. From the moment he first arrived, he had been surprised at how cold it could be in the mornings in this strange Arizona Territory

"Where are we going?" Rob asked. He was barely able to keep his teeth from chattering as he talked. He pulled on his boots, and the shock of the cold leather against feet which had been warmed from the bed covers almost made his toes draw up.

"Big Jake thinks there may be some beeves up in Candlestick Draw, 'n he wants us to ride up there 'n take a look aroun'."

"Do we have to find them in the middle of the night?" Rob asked. "Won't they still be there in the daytime?"

"Ha," Curly said. "That's a pretty good joke. It'll be daytime before we get there," he said. "Maybe you just don't know how far away this here Candlestick Draw is."

"How far is it?"

"It's nigh on to ten miles, 'n that's all cross-country," Curly said. "Now shake a leg, Ed's got us some biscuits 'n bacon and hot coffee, that is, iffen I can drag your tenderfoot hide over there 'fore he throws it out."

"You mean Ed got up early just for us?" Rob asked. "He must be something special."

"Yeah," Curly said. "I'm glad you noticed it as some-thin' special. Most tenderfeet don't, you know. They figger they got it comin', 'n they ain't grateful when they get it, 'n they raise Cain when they don't. But the fac' is, you won't hardly get a belly robber on any other spread to do that. No sir, we are lucky we have someone like Ed Reynolds, 'cause he is somethin' special indeed."

Outside the bunkhouse the dark sky stretched over their heads like the vaulted ceiling of a great cathedral.

Except for the blazing of thousands of stars, the sky was forebodingly silent and empty.

Rob looked up at the sky. The stars ranged from the very brightest, which were white and blinking almost like beacons, to the dimmest, which were no more than a suggestion of stardust shimmering mysteriously in the trackless distance.

The Big House, the foreman's house, and the bunkhouse were all dark. Only the cookhouse showed a light, and it was just a small, square patch of yellow which splashed out from the kitchen window as if keeping some lonely vigil.

Rob looked toward the foreman's house. He knew which window was Melanie's bedroom, and he knew that just on the other side of that window, burrowed down snug and warm in her bed was the most beautiful, most intriguing woman he had ever met.

"I know exactly what you're thinkin', pard," Curly said.

"What?" Rob asked, shocked by the intrusion. Did Curly really know what he was thinking? Had he thought aloud? "You know what I'm thinking?"

"I sure do. Would you like me to tell you?"

"If you think you can," Rob said. He didn't really want Curly telling him what he was thinking. Not if Curly was right. Still, he must play the game if he didn't wish to make matters worse, so he had to pretend that he wanted Curly to guess.

"I seen you lookin' toward Miss Melanie's room," Curly said. "You was lookin' over there, 'n all the time you was thinkin' what a shame it is that a girl like that's gonna marry up with a galoot like Les Garrison."

"Yeah, you're right. I am thinking what a shame it is she's planning on marrying Les Garrison. What do you suppose she sees in a man like that, anyway?" Rob asked.

"He's got money," Curly said.

"Is that all?"

"That's important to a girl."

"There are some things that should be more important," Rob said.

"What could be more important?"

"Whether or not she loves him, for one," Rob suggested. "It would seem to me like that would be the most important thing of all."

"Well," Curly chuckled, "you couldn't hardly expect someone like Miss Melanie to love a no-'count cowpuncher, could you? Let alone marry one."

"I... I guess not," Rob said. "Still, a man could have some hope."

"Rob, don't tell me that you..." Curly started, then he stopped. "Damn me if I don't think you haven't gone and done it."

"Gone and done what?" Rob asked.

"I don't know why I expected you to be any different from any other cowpoke, though. I've knowed Melanie from the time she was borned. Onliest thang is, most ever' one knows how unlikely it is, so all they do is just look at her like she's some sort of princess or somethin' as long as they got enough sense not to expect nothin' to come of it."

"Except for Les Garrison," Rob suggested.

"Beg pardon?"

"Les Garrison expects something to come of it, and it's going to," Rob suggested.

"Yeah," Curly said bitterly. "Except for Les Garrison. But then, they ain't nobody that's ever accused Les Garrison o' playin' by anybody's rules 'ceptin' his own."

They were talking as they walked, and had crossed to the cookhouse by now. Curly pushed the door open, then they walked inside. A warm, cheery glow came from the kitchen, not only from the lantern Ed had lit, but also from the wood-burning stove, which was roaring and popping and filling the little cookhouse with its inviting heat. The rich aroma of coffee and frying bacon permeated the room.

"Ed, damn me if you don't make gettin' outa bed worth it in the mornin'," Curly said as the two men walked back to the kitchen and warmed their hands over the roaring stove.

Ed laughed. "Well, biscuits 'n coffee will work pretty good iffen you ain't leavin' anythin' pretty in bed behind you," he said.

"What's a poor cowboy like us ever gonna leave in bed, 'ceptin' a little trail dirt?" Curly asked, pouring himself a cup of coffee. "I was just tryin' to explain that to my educated pard here as we was walkin' over to the cook shack."

"Friend, don't tell me you took on a cowboy's life without understandin' all there was to know about it," Ed said as he took the strips of bacon up from the pan. Into the bacon drippings he sprinkled a handful of flour and some milk, and a moment later produced a bowl of gravy for Curly and Rob to put over their biscuits. Both men helped themselves to generous amounts.

"I figure it's never too late to learn," Rob said.

"Well, now, that truly is a fact," Ed agreed. "A fella can always learn, that is, iffen he's of a mind to. But it 'pears to me you could'a picked somethin' else to learn besides cowboyin'. Like maybe saddle-makin', or haircuttin' or train-engineerin' or some such. There sure as hell ain't no future in cowboyin'."

"Sure'n someone told me that self-same thing when I was young," Curly said, cheerfully slurping some coffee. "I didn't pay no never-mind to it, 'n I don' reckon Rob is goin' to neither. I reckon on that point, he's about as bull-headed as I was."

"Well," Ed chuckled. "Iffen he's bull-headed, then he's already halfway to bein' a cowboy. I ain't never met a one what had good sense."

"'Ceptin' maybe Big Jake," Curly put in.

"Now that's a fact," Ed agreed. "Big Jake is one of the finest men I've ever knowed. But then, they just ain't many men like him, cowboy or no."

"Ed rode with Big Jake back in Texas, didn't you? Them two was in the war together."

"You and Ed fought in the Civil War?" Rob asked.

"Up North they called it a Civil War," Ed said. "We called it the War Between the States. It was a noble cause we rode for. But that cause is dead now, just like lots of good men who fought it."

"That was a long time ago," Rob said.

"Yeah, I reckon it was," Ed replied. "It's been more'n twenty years since I last heard the sound of battle."

"Do you miss it?"

Ed chuckled. "Now that's a damn fool question to ask of a man. Who would miss battle? But I tell you what I do miss. I miss the men we was with then. War brings out the best in men." Ed was quiet for a moment. "And the worst, too, I reckon, for I seen both kinds."

Rob shivered. "I'm glad I was much too young to have experienced that. If I have my way I'll never go to any war."

Ed looked at Rob, then gave him another helping of bacon.

"You're all right, son," Ed said. "Lots of young guys

are all full of piss 'n vinegar, spoutin' off how they wisht they'd been aroun' to fight. You got a little more sense than that, I see."

Ed's acceptance of him pleased Rob very much, and he was secretly glad that he had such a man working for him.

He wished he could tell him that now, only this wasn't the opportune time. But that time would come. Until then, Rob would just watch, learn, and wait.

10

They had been riding for the better part of an hour and it was still dark. In fact, it was even darker, because a cover of clouds had moved down from the mountains, and the clouds blotted out the moon and the stars. Objects that had been clearly discernible in the moonlight now became nothing but mysterious shapes and shadows.

"It's gonna rain soon," Curly said. "Did you bring your slicker?"

"Yes," Rob answered. He had learned the hard way how quickly a rainstorm could build up in the mountains, so that a perfectly clear day could turn into a downpour in a matter of minutes. He had been caught out without his slicker once, and he vowed never to be caught short again.

"Look over there," Curly said, pointing to a shadow which became a small cabin. "Do you see that buildin'?"

"Yes, I see it," Rob said, barely able to make it out in the darkness. "What is it, someone's house?"

"Yeah, maybe your house," Curly said.

"My house?" Rob answered with a surprised gasp. Had Curly discovered Rob's secret?

Curly chuckled. "It'll be your house if you're ever caught out and need one. Actually, it's a line shack. In the wintertime, when the snow is deep 'n we're out ridin' the herd, we spend a lot of time in line shacks. It's easier than tryin' to get back into the bunkhouse ever' night."

"Are there many of them?"

"Oh, 'bout twenty or so, I would say," Curly answered. "Some of 'em is kept up better'n others. We try 'n keep 'em all stocked with a little food, but ever' now 'n then a drifter, or an Injun comes through 'n cleans it out." Curly rubbed his chin. "Les complains that it's costin' the ranch a lot of money, 'n he said we should shoot anybody we ever catch lootin' one of the places. But the truth is, I've been an uninvited guest in line shacks myself a few times in my day. It's sort of an unwritten law that a man who is hungry 'n desperate can take shelter for a while iffen he don't abuse it."

"Are they abusing these line shacks?" Rob asked.

"No," Curly answered. "Garrison can't pull that ole' dodge. That ain't where the money is goin'."

"What money?" Rob asked.

"Ah, don't worry about it, pard," Curly said. "It ain't no bother of our'n. We're just the small fish in this kettle of stew. Let the owners, whoever the hell they are, worry about it. If they don't care that Garrison is stealin' 'em blind, why should we?"

Rob was suddenly very attentive. Big Jake had alluded to this same thing. Now he realized more than ever, how fortunate it was that neither of them realized he was the owner. Rob understood that if they knew, their strange sense of honor would prevent them from talking about it to him. Whatever was going on, Rob was going to have to find out on his own hook.

"Are you saying Garrison is a crook?" Rob asked, being careful not to appear too interested.

"Well, I guess there's degrees of being crooked," Curly said. "Truth is, I reckon near 'bout ever' rancher in the West has thrown a long rope at one time or another, prob'ly even includin' Big Jake. The story is that's one o' the reasons why he left Texas."

"A long rope?"

Curly looked at Rob and laughed. "Say, you really don't know much, do you? A long rope is when a cattle rancher sort of accidental like runs another man's cows in with his own. 'Course, it's only accidental if he gets caught. Otherwise, it's just plain smart ranchin'."

"Is that what Garrison and Big Jake are doing? Throwing a long rope?"

"No, there ain't no way Big Jake is in on it," Curly said. "I've know'd Jake for twenty years, 'n while he was more'n likely involved in a few shenanigans whilst he was back 'n Texas, he was dealin' with the thievin' carpetbaggers then, 'n he had ever' right to be, so iffen he was gettin' his own cows back, you can't rightly say that it was rustlin'. Anyhow, in all the time he's been out here in Arizona, he's never done nothin' ag'in them that own the Turquoise."

"Do you think Garrison's, uh, how did you put it? Throwing a long rope?"

"Yeah," Curly replied. "And the thing is, Garrison ain't none too particular where his rope lands. You see, he ain't stealin' from his neighbors, he's stealin' from the hand that's feedin' him. He's takin' Turquoise cows for his own."

"How can he do that?" Rob asked.

"They's lots of ways of doin' it," Curly said. "One way is to sell five hunnert head 'n only report four hunnert. Another way is to report losin' ten to twenty more cows than was actual lost in a winter blizzard. Fac' is, I got me a hunch these here cows we're goin' after today might be somethin' like that."

"What do you mean?"

"Well, they ain't no real reason for these cows to be in Candlestick Draw, 'lessen they was put there to wait out the winter. I 'spect they already been counted dead. Yes, sir, whatever we find up here, we will sell, 'n you can make book that all the money these cows make is goin' to wind up in Les Garrison's pockets."

"Didn't you say Big Jake sent us after these cows?" Rob said.

"Yes, he did."

"Then that means he must be in on it, doesn't it? I mean, if he knows where the cows are."

"I don't know, pard," Curly said. "I don't want to think that, but I just don't know."

Rob recalled the conversation he and Jake had when he asked to be relieved of the handyman jobs. Jake had protested his innocence then, protesting even before an accusation was made. Did he, perhaps, protest too much?

"What do you think, Curly? Are we helping Big Jake and Les Garrison rustle these cows right now?"

Curly pulled his hat off and rubbed his hair for a moment.

"Now, pard, I just don't have the answer to that," he said. "On the one hand, I don't see how Big Jake could be foreman here 'n not know what's goin' on. Most particular, since he's got some shadow on his own trail. But that was a long time ago, 'n ever' one is entitled to keep a door closed on his past iffen he's of a mind to. Besides which, as long as I've know'd 'im, 'n that's a long time, Big Jake has rode nothin' but a straight path. I know I ain't never met no man who was straighter with me. 'N I'll be honest with you, Rob, it would a sore disappointment to me iffen I was to find that he was in some sort of trouble now. But the truth is I'd have to be on his side, no matter what."

"You would defend him, even if the owner had proof that Big Jake was stealing from him?" Rob asked. "You'd still side with Big Jake?"

"When I got throwed from a horse a few years back and was busted up somethin' awful, it wa'nt the owner who patched me up," Curly said. "It was Big Jake. Yes, sir, if push ever come to shove, you'd find me in Big Jake's corner."

Rob was quiet for several minutes after that. This was something he would have to think about. He recalled an incident that occurred a few years earlier, when during the summer break of his education at Harvard, he sailed on one of his grandfather's ships.

As he was doing now, he had withheld his identity to the officers and crew of the *USS Success,* a screw propelled steam ship belonging to the Barringer Shipping Company. Rob had used his mother's maiden name, Prouty, and was sailing as an Able Bodied.

Though not one stalk of cotton was grown in England, England produced half the world's supply of cotton cloth, and that was the cargo that the *Success* was carrying back to the U.S. However, the *Success* made an unscheduled stop in Canada, where almost ten percent of the cloth was off-loaded. When they reached Boston, the captain claimed a loss to natural elements, of the same amount of cloth that had been off-loaded in Canada.

Rob reported the unauthorized transaction to his grandfather, and the ship's captain was fired.

Now, it would seem that the same sort of shenanigans were taking place on the Turquoise, the only difference being that it wasn't his grandfather, or his father's business, it was his own. And the question was, what was he going to do about it?

For one thing, he wasn't going to jump to conclusions. As an ordinary cowhand, he enjoyed near invisibility, and he would use that to determine if he was being cheated, and if so, who was the guilty party?

He hoped that it wasn't Jake. He liked Jake, and it wasn't just because Jake was Melanie's father.

THE MOON and stars which had shined so brightly overhead when Rob and Curly left were gone now, to be replaced by the clouds that had moved down from the mountains.

The wind freshened, bringing on its breath the rain Curly had warned of a few moments earlier. Off in the distance, there was a long, low rumble. Curly reached into his saddle roll and pulled out his poncho, and Rob followed suit.

"I told you so, pard. We're about to get wet," Curly called. "You're gonna find yourself wishin' you was back doin' chores. At least you wouldn't have to be out in weather like this."

A long, jagged streak of lightning split the night sky, and for just an instant the rugged terrain around them was brightly illuminated. It reminded Rob of a photograph, a split second of time lifted out of the continuum and frozen for an eternity.

The rain began then. At first it was no more than a few fat, heavy drops. Then there was more and more still, until finally the rain was cascading down in sheets.

The rain gushed down as they rode. It slashed into them in stinging sheets, and ran in cold rivulets off the folds and creases of their ponchos. It blew in gusts across the trail in front of them and drummed wickedly into the rocks and the trees around them.

Curly held his hand up, giving a signal for Rob to stop. He said something, but Rob couldn't hear him.

"What?" Rob shouted.

Curly had to cup his hand around his mouth and shout in order to be heard above the storm. He pointed to a draw in front of him.

"You go on up to the end of this draw," he shouted. "You'll find a line shack there. Go on in and get out of the rain. When it gets light, ride down the draw and see if there are any cows. If you find any, push 'em on through." Curly was shouting, but his voice was thin against the wind and the rain.

"What are you going to do?" Rob shouted back.

"This draw wanders around for a bit, then it comes out about another mile down the trail. When you push 'em through, that's where they'll come out. I'll be waitin' there for 'em."

"Do you have a place to get out of the rain?" Rob shouted.

"Better'n you," Curly replied, smiling broadly. "Why do you think I sent you in here?"

Rob returned Curly's smile. "I don't know," he said. "Maybe I just thought you were being friendly."

"I'm only friendly when it don't cost me nothin'," Curly replied with a laugh. He slapped his chap-covered legs against the side of his horse and rode on.

Rob watched Curly for just a moment, then he started up his end of the draw. It was a long, narrow, twisting canyon, filled with rocks which had tumbled down from the steep walls, and cut with cross ravines and gullies which made its transit difficult. The fact that it was dark and storming made it even more difficult, so when Rob finally emerged at the other end and saw the dark shadow of the line shack, he was more than a little relieved.

There was a small lean-to horse shelter to one side of the shack, and Rob led his horse into the shelter and tied it off.

"Sorry you can't come in with me," he said. "But you'll be just fine here."

Rob went inside, found a kerosene lantern on a wooden table and lit it. A soft golden bubble of light filled the room, and he looked around to examine his temporary quarters. There was a small wood-burning stove in the middle of the room and a coffeepot on the stove. Rob wished he had some coffee, but short of putting the pot outside to catch the rain, he had no idea of how he would get water. Finally, he gave up that idea, but he did decide to build a fire. He figured it would be an hour or so before he started after the cows, so he might as well try to warm himself.

Within moments the fire was roaring, and already the room was beginning to warm. Then Rob got an idea. Why not take off his clothes and hang them over a chair near the stove? They would dry, or nearly dry, and even if it was still raining when he started after the cows, he would at least have had the advantage of being out of the wet things for a short time.

AFTER THE RAIN STOPPED, Rob rode away from the shack with the intention of meeting up with Curly.

"Rob?" Curly called out. "Rob, is that you?"

"Yes."

"Where you been, boy? I thought you were going to push the cows out to me."

"I'm sorry," Rob said. "I guess it just took me a little longer to get up here than I thought."

"Ah, that's all right," Curly said. "This is your first time. I should'a taken this part and let you wait at the other end. Come on, I spotted them. Let's move 'em out."

"Where are they?"

"They're back in the blind draw there," Curly said. "Damnedest thing."

"What?"

"It looks like they was put in there of a purpose. Rob, them are rustled cattle sure as God created you and me."

11

Melanie's reasoning told her that Les Garrison was the right man for her and if she was being coldly dispassionate, she realized that it could well be because she was interested in Les's money and position. No, she realized, it wasn't really Les's money, it was the ranch itself, and the fact that he managed it. If she married Les Garrison, she would always be a part of it, and so would her father, even when he was too old to work anymore.

Melanie had left the house shortly after sunrise this morning, and rode out over the ranch, which was now rain-washed and sparkling bright under the morning sun. Though she saw it every day, she never had a day in which she didn't find some new aspect of its beauty to appreciate. The ranch was so big that it was like a kaleidoscope. One never got the same perspective twice, even if looking at the same view.

This morning, for example, she was struck by the sight of the droplets of water clinging to the bushes and lying on the petals of the wild flowers. At this precise moment the sun was at just the right angle to catch the droplets so that there were millions of diamond-like prisms spread out before her, breaking the morning sunbeams into a rainbow spectrum of brilliant color. The sight was positively breathtaking.

Melanie stopped and stared at the scene, enraptured by its beauty. Unfortunately, it only lasted for a few moments, because the continued rise of the sun gradually bent the angle of the falling light until the diamonds disappeared. How could she even consider leaving this place?

ROB HAD NOT BEEN to this part of the ranch before, and he looked around as he and Curly pushed the cattle back to the main herd. How magnificent it was! The sun was well up now, shedding a vast, clear, golden light over the entire range. This part of the ranch looked like a beautiful park, covered with sun-bleached grass and dotted with clumps of trees in mottled shades of green. Mountains rose in majestic grandeur all around.

"Curly," Rob said. He took in the surrounding country-side with a sweep of his hand. "Curly, don't you just love it?"

Curly laughed. "I reckon I do, pard," he said. "I reckon I do."

Curly watched Rob. He had never seen any tenderfoot take hold so fast, nor had he ever met a tenderfoot he liked as quickly. Most tenderfoot cowpokes lost interest in adventure as soon as hard work started. Not Rob. He was willing to pull his share and then some.

There was a moment this morning when Curly was a little concerned, however. He had waited in the shack until the rain stopped, then he went to the head of the draw to wait for Rob to push the cattle down to him. When the cattle didn't come, he rode up the draw to see what was wrong. Curly reached the cattle, but still saw no sight of Rob. He was concerned that Rob had gotten lost or, worse, had fallen asleep in the cabin. He was just about to ride back and see what was keeping him when he saw him arrive. Curly breathed a sigh of relief then, not because the work would have been too much for him to handle by himself, but because he had not wanted to be disappointed in the man he had come to like. Let the others tease him about being a tenderfoot all they wanted. Curly had ridden with a lot of men, but seldom had he encountered a man he thought more of than Rob Barringer.

HAVING ENJOYED her morning ride and exploration of the ranch, Melanie returned to the compound where the buildings stood.

"Where have you been?" Les asked. There was a proprietary degree of sharpness to his voice which first surprised, and then angered Melanie.

"I wasn't aware that I had to report my every movement to you," she replied indignantly.

Melanie's anger was genuine, for she really didn't believe Les had any right to demand an accounting of her whereabouts.

Then Les saw that she was angry and he suddenly realized that he might have overstepped his bounds, so he quickly recanted.

"I'm sorry, Melanie," he apologized. "I didn't mean to be so harsh. It's just that I was worried about you. Your father said you weren't there when he got up this morning, and I had no idea where you could have gone."

"I am my own person, and I will not answer to you for my every move, either now or after we're married."

"Melanie, I know you are a headstrong person. I think one of the things I like about you is your spirit. And perhaps I am being a bit overly concerned. But I think you should understand that once we are married, I have every intention of being aware of your whereabouts at all times. After all, you will be my wife, and as my wife, you will occupy a position of some responsibility. Don't forget, I am a man of considerable importance. You won't be the daughter of a mere foreman anymore. You will be the wife of a cattleman. A cattleman's wife has an obligation not only to her husband, but to her social position. I shall certainly expect you to conduct yourself accordingly."

"A mere foreman? You call my father a *mere* foreman? What are you but a glorified foreman?" Melanie asked angrily. She surprised herself by the sharpness of her response, but she was stung by what she considered to be a derisive reference to her father.

"I would hardly call my position that of a foreman, my dear," Garrison said.

"What would you call it?" Melanie asked. "After all, you don't own Turquoise Ranch, you just run it."

"Perhaps I don't own it," Garrison said. "But I do control it, and that is practically the same thing. The fate of this ranch, its owners, and everyone on it, depends upon me and the decisions I make. Your father's position, as well as the position of all the cowboys, is subject to my approval, or," he added ominously, "my disapproval."

"Are you threatening my father's position here?" Melanie asked.

"Melanie, have I made such a threat? You know that as long as we are married, your father's position as foreman of this ranch is safe."

As long as we are married? Melanie thought. There it is again, an implied threat. Does that mean she has to marry him to insure her father's job? No, surely not. Perhaps it was just her own sense of guilt that was causing her to think this way. After all, as they were engaged, Les did have the right to be concerned about her. And she had left just after dawn, and that could cause someone to wonder.

"I'm sorry," she said. "I have a secret place I go to sometimes. I've been going to it for years. I don't suppose it's all that big of a secret. Papa knows about it. I went there this morning and that is what caused me to be late. I didn't realize anyone would be worrying about me."

Les softened before Melanie's new strategy, and he smiled at her. "That's all right," he said. "It's just that I wanted to find you because I'm expecting some important people for lunch. This will give you your first opportunity to perform some of the social functions which will be expected of you after we're married. I want you to come to lunch with us. Will you?"

"Of course I will," Melanie said, smiling sweetly. She was glad that the subject had been changed, and though she really didn't want to join him for lunch, she felt as if she didn't have any choice. She felt that she owed him that.

MELANIE DIDN'T CARE for Les's guests. They were identified to her as important cattle buyers, and they wore their titles as badges of authority.

"Yes, thank you," one of them answered in response to a question. "We have enjoyed a great deal of success over the past year. You might say we have had a banner year."

"Another year this good, and we can get out of the business," the other one said.

"Why would you want to leave a business that is obviously so successful?" Les asked.

"Why? You work and live around these smelly animals, you deal with the type of man who becomes a cowboy, and you ask why? The cattle business is a good business to make money, especially if you are as... shall we say, lucky... as we have been. But I certainly don't like the people who are associated with the business. For the most part I find them to be among the lowest specimens of life. They are unwashed, uneducated, and uncouth."

That was not the only derogatory comment made about ranching in general and cowboys in particular. Several other times during the course of the conversation, they said things that implied their disdain for the cowboys and others who honestly toiled for a living. Melanie heard about as much as she could take, and she was tempted to ask them if they thought they could have the success they were enjoying if it weren't for the cowboys who made everything go. They were obviously enjoying their success. They were both dressed in expensive suits and tooled-leather boots.

One of the men was very large, and rolls of fat spilled across his tight collar. His suit, though expensive, was too small, and he was sweating, though Melanie did not believe it was actually that warm. He kept sticking his finger between his collar and his neck, pulling it out, as if trying to get room to breathe. He had close-set, beady eyes, and Melanie could feel them burning into her as he watched her hungrily all through the meal. Melanie knew that the hunger in his eyes wasn't for food, and the thought of that made her flesh crawl.

The fat man's name was Beaty. The other man was cadaverously thin with sunken cheeks and deep, dark brown eyes. He had only looked at Melanie once, and that was when they were introduced. Where Beaty's eyes were clouded with undisguised lust, the thin man, whose name was Holman, had eyes that were as expressionless as those of a dead fish.

He seemed to have an interest in only one thing, and that was cattle.

"What a beautiful creature your fiancée is," Beaty wheezed over a glass of wine. "Don't you think so, Mr. Holman?"

"What?" Holman asked. He looked up from some papers which had occupied a prominent position by his plate all during lunch. "Oh, yes, she is lovely." Holman moved his facial muscles in what may have been a smile, but he returned immediately to his work. He was a cold fish, but in fact Melanie much preferred his indifference to her, over Beaty's long, lustful glances. She also didn't particularly care for the way they were speaking of her in the third person, as if she weren't even there.

"My dear, have you ever been to the city?" Beaty asked.

"I've been to Flagstaff several times," Melanie answered.

"Flagstaff? Oh, no, my dear. I mean a real city. Denver, perhaps. Or San Francisco."

"No," Melanie said. "I've never been there."

"Too bad. A lovely creature like you would have a wonderful time. There are so many things to do. You could go to the ballet, the opera, the theater... or you could just visit the fine restaurants. I am a connoisseur of fine restaurants. Do you know what that means?"

"You eat a lot?" Melanie said innocently.

Les laughed, and so did Beaty. Only Holman remained expressionless.

"Oh, you sweet thing," Beaty said. "As a matter of fact, you can, no doubt, tell from my appearance that I do eat a lot as you so adroitly put it. But in truth, a connoisseur is a person with exquisite taste, possessed of an acute discrimination when it comes to making selections. If you were to visit a restaurant with me, you may be assured it would be a wonderful experience for you."

"Oh, well, I think Les would have something to say about that," Melanie said.

"Mr. Beaty is a business associate, my dear. If he chose to take you to a restaurant, I would hope you would be honored to accept the invitation."

Melanie looked at Les in surprise. Did he know what he was saying? Didn't he realize that Mr. Beaty had more than visiting a restaurant on his mind? Couldn't Les see the lust in Beaty's eyes? Or, worse, did he realize it but disregard it because Beaty was a business associate, and he didn't want to offend him? Was this what Les meant when he said that as a cattleman's wife, she would have certain responsibilities?

"Mr. Garrison, may we get back to business?" Holman asked.

"Yes, of course," Les replied.

Holman went on, "I have here the invoices from the last shipment. As you can see, everything is all accounted for, including the loss in transit, etcetera."

"You are talking about the invoices for the Colorado Cattle Company?" Les asked.

Holman looked up sharply, then he glanced over toward Melanie. In that one glance she saw more expression in his face than she had seen at any time since he arrived.

"I would prefer not to talk about that in front of..."

"Don't worry about her," Les interrupted easily.

"I don't know," Holman said. "I'm not sure it is a good thing to discuss the business of the company at all. It is especially dangerous to discuss it around outsiders."

"I told you, don't worry about her," Garrison said again, more sharply than before. "She is not exactly an outsider. She is Jake Dunford's daughter. Obviously, she has her father's best interests at heart. That means she won't do anything to jeopardize our business."

"You are certain she understands the consequences of any indiscretion?"

"What consequences?" Melanie asked, confused now by the direction of the conversation.

"I will see that she understands," Garrison said. "Now that that is settled, what about new business? Have you any new business for me?"

"Yes, as a matter of fact I do," Holman answered. "We have a requirement of three thousand head on your next shipment."

"Three thousand?" Garrison said. He whistled. "I don't know, that may be a little larger than I can handle. You've never taken more than two hundred and fifty head before."

"Yes," Holman said, "but now we have a government contract to sell cattle to the San Carlos Apache Indian Reservation, down near Phoenix. We must meet that quota or we will lose the contract. You can see that it is imperative that we get all the beef. It is preferable to get it all from one source. We were hoping you would be that source."

Les pulled out a long, thin cheroot, bit off the tip and put it in his mouth. Melanie lit a match and held it to the end of the cigar.

"Uhmm, thanks," Garrison said, puffing on the cigar until it was lit. He pulled the cigar from his mouth, and with his head ringed in a cloud of aromatic blue smoke, he looked at Holman and Beaty.

"That's quite an order. I'm not certain I can come up with three thousand cows," he said. "The losses we have been reporting back East have been exceptionally large as it is. Something like this would just be too much."

"I think you will find that this deal is worth it," Holman said. "We are willing to pay top price."

"Oh?" Garrison said with interest. "What would that be?"

"Twenty-five dollars a head," Beaty said.

"That would be seventy-five thousand dollars," Holman added.

Les smiled. "Seventy-five thousand dollars, you say?"

"All in cash," Beaty put in. "Untraceable. Provided, of course, that the cattle you provide us are the same. That is to say, untraceable."

Les put the cigar back in his mouth and cocked it up at a jaunty angle.

"Gentlemen, I think you have just found your untraceable cattle," he said, smiling broadly. "Shall we drink a toast to it?"

12

It was late in the evening of that same day before Rob and Curly returned from their job. Big Jake invited both of them in for coffee, and Curly accepted gratefully, but Rob mumbled some excuse as to why he couldn't come and he left Curly to make the report.

"What's the matter with Rob?" Big Jake asked as he poured coffee for the two of them. "He acted like he didn't want to come in."

"Melanie, girl, come join us," Curly said.

"Well, I suppose I can sit with you two for a while," she said.

"Oh ho, listen to that now, will you?" Curly said. "Time was when you was a little girl, I couldn't keep you away from me."

"You were my hero then," Melanie said as a smile crossed her face.

"Uh huh, 'n I ain't no more? Well, that I can understand. Little girls grow up to be big girls 'n then they put away childish things. I reckon heroes are one of 'em." Curly took a drink of coffee from his cup and eyed her over the rim. "They is one thing I can't understand, though, girl, 'n that's why you got somethin' agin' Rob. Iffen you ask me, he is as fine a cowboy as ever forked a horse, though truth be told, he ain't really no cowboy. He's somethin' much finer'n any cowboy I've ever knowed, which makes it hard to understand what you got ag'in him."

Melanie looked shocked. "Why, Curly, I don't have anything against Rob. Why would you think such a thing?"

"It's just somethin' I've noticed," Curly said. "I see it in the way he acts. He don't want to talk none about you, 'n all the while we was comin' back here, he was actin' real strange, liken as if he was afraid he was gonna run into you when we come to talk to Big Jake. Why, I bet he asked me a hunnert times iffen I didn't think I could make the report without him, 'cause he didn't want to upset you, by bein' around you. Now what I want to know is, why would it upset you for him to be around?"

"Daughter, have you taken a dislike to Rob for some reason? Does it upset you for him to be around?" Jake asked.

Melanie looked down at the floor. "No, Papa, not exactly."

"Not exactly? What do you mean by not exactly? That's no answer."

"It's just that I fear Rob might…" Melanie paused in the middle of her explanation.

"He might what?"

"Papa, Rob seems to harbor some hope that… something… could exist between the two of us. Of course, such an idea is ridiculous, but he seems to harbor it, nonetheless."

"Why is it so ridiculous?" Jake asked. "For my way of

thinkin', Rob Barringer is a good man. Curly has vouched for him, and you can't get a higher recommendation in my book."

"Why thank you, boss," Curly said, genuinely moved by Jake's endorsement of his judgment.

"Papa, you know why it's ridiculous," Melanie said. "I'm engaged to Les Garrison. Or have you forgotten?"

"No," Jake said. "I'm not likely to forget that. Have you?"

"Have I? What do you mean?"

"I mean how can you account for Rob's strange belief that there might be somethin' between the two of you, unless you've led him on a bit?"

"I don't know," Melanie said quietly. "I can't explain that."

"Well now, boss, truth to be told, Miss Melanie may have nothin' to do with it anyway. For all that I like the man, I got to say that sometimes there don't seem to be no accountin' for how Rob acts," Curly said. "He's about the most different person I ever laid eyes on."

"What do you mean?" Big Jake asked. "In what way is he different?"

"Different from all the other cowboys I've ever know'd," Curly said. "Now you take his education. He's a educated man, I know that," Curly said. "He sure don't look educated—I mean him bein' so big 'n all—but he's educated all right. He's always talkin' 'bout things he's read in books, 'n you know it takes a educated man to be able to talk about things in books. And strong? Boss, I always thought you was the strongest man I'd ever seen, but Rob can go you one better. Have you heard about what he did with the tie-bar offen the grain wagon?"

"No," Big Jake said. "What about it?"

"The other day, we was usin' the grain wagon to haul

some barbed wire. Well sir, we was up at Tooley Creek where all them boulders has been washed down from the mountains, don't you know, and the wagon hit a rock. The driver had just whipped the team up to make the upgrade, so when it hit the rock, well, the tie-bar got bent up somethin' awful. You know how downright hard it is to straighten one of them things out. You got to heat it up in a fire, then you got to pound it out over a forge. Well, Rob didn't know that, 'n when one of the boys, just jokin' mind you, told Rob to straighten the tie-bar out, well, Rob commenced to do just that!"

"Are you telling me that Rob Barringer straightened a bent tie-bar?" Jake asked, impressed by the feat of strength.

"He did just that," Curly said. "Ole Rob just pulled that tie-bar offen the wagon, stuck one end of it down in a rock crevice, then he pulled on the other end with both hands until it straightened out pretty as you please, just liken it was in the first place. You should'a seen him, boss. He took off his shirt and he had muscles poppin' out on top of muscles."

Big Jake let out a soft sigh of surprise. "He must be one strong son of a bitch," he said.

"Ain't that the truth, though?" Curly answered, and Melanie noted some pride in Curly's voice, as if he were sharing in Rob's accomplishments because he was Rob's best friend.

"But, now here's the kicker. He's always doin' things like that without givin' it a second thought. It's as if his strength comes so natural to him that it don't seem nothin' unusual to him."

"I must confess to a degree of curiosity over Mr. Barringer's background myself," Big Jake said. "He comes here from the East, he is educated and, though I don't know for sure, I get the idea that he is from a fine family. Most young men like that fold when the going gets tough. Mr. Barringer has stayed on. There's a mystery there all right, but I sure don't know what it is. I would be very interested to find out."

"Please," Melanie finally said in exasperation. "Must we always talk about Rob Barringer? It seems like ever since he arrived, I've been seeing him or hearing about him. I'd like to just get him out of my mind for a while!"

Big Jake and Curly looked at Melanie with some surprise over her sudden outburst. When Melanie realized what a thing she had made over it, she glanced quickly down to the floor, and her cheeks flamed in embarrassment.

"I mean, you can talk about him if you want to, but I thought a man's personal life was his own. If Rob Barringer wanted people to know more about him, he would tell them."

"You know, Curly, the girl is right," Big Jake said. "I got things in my own past I don't particularly like to talk about, so I reckon we got no business speculatin' about Rob's past."

"No, I guess not," Curly said.

"Tell me about your job this morning," Big Jake said, changing the subject. "Did everything go all right?"

"Yeah," Curly said. "Boss, you know they was near on to a hunnert head of cattle we caught up there in Candlestick Draw."

"One hundred head you say?" Big Jake whistled. "We're lucky they didn't die in there. That would've been three thousand dollars lost, right there."

Melanie looked at her father in surprise.

"Yeah, well, here is the funny thing, boss. Them cows was as good off in there as the ones we was runnin' out on the range. Fac' is, someone had took the trouble to damn up a creek 'n send some water into the draw. Why, them cows had ever'thin' they needed in there. It was almost like they was put in there of a pure purpose."

Big Jake looked at Curly for a long, musing moment.

"What are you trying to say, Curly?"

"It looked to me like some rustlers might have took the notion to cut out about a hunnert head. For some reason they couldn't get 'em off the ranch, so they run 'em into Candlestick Draw, aimin' to come back later 'n pick 'em up. Leastwise, that's my way of thinkin' on the subject."

"That's a possibility," Big Jake agreed. "That's certainly a possibility."

Curly set his coffee cup down on a nearby table and stood up, then stretched.

"Boss, it ain't that I don't enjoy jawin' with you, you unnerstan', but I gotta tell you, I'm one tired cowpoke."

"Yes, Curly, well, you go ahead and turn in," Big Jake said. "You put in a good day's work today. And tell Rob that goes for him, too."

"Right, boss. Good night," Curly said. "And good night to you, too, Miss Melanie."

Melanie watched her father walk to the door with Curly, then after Curly was gone, she spoke to him.

"Papa, what did you mean when you said that those one hundred head of cattle were worth three thousand dollars?"

Big Jake chuckled. "Now you're beginning to see why Turquoise Ranch is worth so much money, are you? Well, it's very simple. One head will bring about thirty dollars. Sometimes it's a little more, but when you consider the attrition rate during shipment, one thing and another, you can pretty well count on about thirty dollars a head. Turquoise Ranch is probably running around twenty thousand head, so there is more than half a million dollars in stock alone, let alone the value of the rangeland and its buildings."

"Are you sure about that, Papa? About the price of cattle, I mean."

Jake walked over to a roll top desk and opened it. He picked up a small printed circular.

"Here is an offering from the Southern Pacific Railroad," he said. "They're paying thirty-one dollars at the railhead in Flagstaff. If a fella wanted to shop around, he might be able to beat that, but not by much."

"Would there ever be a reason for someone selling their cattle at twenty-five dollars a head?"

"Perhaps."

"Why would someone do that?"

"If they come by the cows dishonestly, they'll often discount them so that the buyer doesn't ask too many questions."

"Have you ever known anyone to do that?"

Jake frowned at his daughter. "You ask too many questions," he said. "One of these days you may get an answer you don't want to hear."

Suddenly Melanie had a most disquieting thought. Les had told the cattle buyers that he would have her father's best interests at heart. Did that mean that Les and her father were in partnership over some scheme to cheat the owners of Turquoise Ranch? What if the owners found out?

"Papa, why has the owner of this ranch never bothered to come look at it?" Melanie asked.

"Why do you ask that?" Jake asked.

Melanie didn't want to raise her father's suspicions, so she said, "It's just that Turquoise Ranch is so beautiful, surely anyone who owned such a bit of paradise would want to see it."

"I don't guess I can answer that question, darlin', 'cause I don't know who owns it," Jake said. "And the truth is, I don't think Les Garrison even knows."

"But how can that be? Surely he has to report to someone, doesn't he?"

"Yes, of course. But it's just to some lawyers who run things. It's a business, darlin', just like any other business, only in this business we raise and sell cows. So it could be that the ranch is owned by some cattle company, instead of by someone."

"How cold," Melanie said. "How awful to reduce such a beautiful place like Turquoise Ranch to a bunch of numbers in a book."

"Perhaps so," Jake said, "but you fail to understand, darlin'. To you and me, and to those of us who live here, Turquoise Ranch is our home, and we love it. But to the businessman or businessmen who own it, it is simply another investment, like buying stock in a railroad or a shipping line. They know nothing about the ranch except its profit-and-loss picture."

"I'm sure that if I ever meet the owner or owners, I shall not like them," Melanie said.

"It's not important that we like them, darlin'. The only important thing is that they like us."

"Why wouldn't they like us?"

Jake laughed. "Oh, there are a lot of reasons why they may not like us. They may decide that we're mismanaging the place, or they may decide to go out of business altogether. That's why we should save as much as we can, just in case we are ever thrown out."

"You mean a person should get all he can while he can?" Melanie asked.

"I wouldn't have put it in those words, but yes."

Melanie felt a great sadness. Now she knew what Holman meant by the consequence of indiscretion. Les and her father were involved in some scheme to cheat the owners. Her father and the man she was going to marry must be crooks.

After Melanie went to bed, Jake walked over to a liquor cabinet and took out a bottle of whiskey. He poured himself a drink, then sat down to enjoy it. Twenty-five dollars a head, huh? He had to hand it to Les. He was getting a good price on the cattle he was stealing. Most rustlers had to discount their cattle by nearly half. And most rustlers took a greater risk all the way around than Les was taking. Les was taking no risk at all. He was merely cutting cattle out of the owner's herd, and selling them off.

Melanie had never known any other home but the Turquoise Ranch, and she loved it. Now she was engaged to Les Garrison, the ranch manager, and Jake couldn't help but hope that she hadn't agreed to his wedding proposal just because of her love for the ranch.

He looked at his glass and saw that it was empty, and he wondered how long he had been sitting there just thinking. His own rustling days were long past, and he had already paid dearly for them. He hoped he didn't get caught up in Les's scheme.

He would make sure that he didn't.

13

Rob heard the sound of a gun being fired, and when he investigated it, he found Curly out behind the barn. He had set up a row of bottles on the fence railing, and he would draw his pistol, shoot one, return his pistol to his holster draw it, and shoot again.

Rob was impressed with the fact that Curly hadn't missed one shot since he had come out here to see what the shooting was about.

"You're pretty good with that gun," Rob said.

"I'm tolerable, I reckon," Curly said.

"Have you ever had to use it? I mean for real."

"I used it a lot durin' the war. I warn't exactly what you would call a regular soldier. Me 'n Jake, he was a captain then, 'n some few others, was more like a wanderin' aroun' bunch of soldiers, findin' where we could hurt the Yankees the most. 'N more often than not, we'd wind up in some shootin' match that was different from the regular soldiers which was lyin' donwn, 'a shootin' at each other rifles 'n such. We was most always on horses, 'n shootin' from the saddle."

"But that was during the war. I can't help but wonder why you and several of the other hands wear guns all the time," Rob said.

Curly chuckled. "Well, you never can tell when you might run in to a polecat or two."

Curly pulled his gun in a very rapid draw, thumbing the hammer back as he raised it, then firing three quick shots. Three of the remaining bottles were shattered by the bullets.

"Here you go, pardner," Curly said, handing the pistol, butt first, to Rob. "Take a shot at one 'o them bottles that's left, and see what you can do."

"All right," Rob said, taking the pistol.

"Which bottle are you going to shoot at?"

"Well, if I wind up hittin' one of 'em, that'll be the one I was shooting at," Rob said with a little chuckle.

Curly laughed. "All right, I'll give you that."

Rob had never fired a weapon of any sort before. Some of his friends back in Boston were hunters, and others belonged to a club that did skeet shooting, but Rob had never done either.

He raised the pistol, pointed it at the row of bottles, and tried to pull the trigger. Nothing happened.

"This is what you call a single-action pistol," Curly explained. "You have to pull the hammer back between ever' shot."

Rob pulled the hammer back then aimed again. When he pulled the trigger, he was surprised at how the gun bucked in his hand.

Not one of the bottles was hit.

Rob chuckled, as handed the pistol back. "If I'm ever set upon by armed men seeking to bring about my demise, I hope you are with me."

Curly laughed. "Pardner, what you just said sounded

real important, but I don't have nary a idea in hell what it is that you did say."

"I said I want you with me if I'm ever attacked by anyone."

"I'll try to be, pardner, I'll try to be," Curly said.

"By the way, if I would like to take three days off, who would I have to ask? Jake, or Les?"

"I wouldn't ask Les if I was you. More 'n likely that son of a bitch would say no, just out of pure orneriness. Ask Jake, he can give you off. What for are you wantin' off? You ain't the kind of feller that's likely to go inter town 'n throw yourself a three-day drunk."

"I want to take a train down to Phoenix."

"Pardner, it beats me why'n the hell you would want to take a train ride down to Phoenix. The onliest thing Phoenix has that Flagstaff don't is just more of the same, is all."

"I'm sure you're right," Rob said. "It's just that I would like to see it, and with three days off, it seems like a fine opportunity."

"Ha," Curly said. "You'll use up a good portion of the first day just getting there, and the third day just comin' back. Think of how we could put that time to good use in Flagstaff. I sure hope you ain't plannin' on me goin' with you."

"You are certainly welcome to come along if you wish," Rob said.

"No thankee. While you're still ridin' on the train, I'll already be havin' me a fine time in Flagstaff."

ROB WAS certain that Curley would turn down his invitation, and in fact, that was exactly what he wanted him to do. Rob did want to go to Phoenix, but he was not exactly honest with Curly in telling him why he wanted to go. Rob wanted to go to Phoenix so he could wire Morgan, Trevathan, and Daigh without danger of someone finding out who he actually was. He was afraid to send a wire from Flagstaff because Flagstaff was so small that it would be impossible for him to hide his business. Phoenix was larger, and farther away, thus assuring him some measure of privacy.

And Curly had been right about the length of time it would take him to get there. It hadn't taken an entire day, but he had boarded the train at seven o'clock in the morning, and it was nearly three o'clock in the afternoon when he arrived.

He was somewhat surprised at how hot it was in Phoenix. Rob had grown used to the cooler climes of Flagstaff, and he wasn't quite prepared for the blistering heat. He braced himself to walk from the shade of the car shed out into the bright Arizona sun.

An old Mexican woman was operating a taco stand right across the street from the station. She didn't have any teeth and she kept her mouth closed so tightly that her chin and nose nearly touched. A swarm of flies buzzed around the steaming kettles, drawn by the pungent aromas of meat and sauce. She worked with quick, deft fingers, rolling the spicy ingredients into tortillas, then wrapping them up in old newspaper as she handed them to her customers.

Rob walked on down the street, taking in the sights and sounds of Phoenix. The city was undergoing a transition from a sleepy cow town of the Old West into a bustling city of the future. Electric trolleys whirred down the dual set of tracks in the center of the street, clanging their bells impatiently at the horses and carriages that had the temerity to get in their way. Both sides of the street were lined with poles which stretched wires along the length of the street, carrying telegraph service as well as electricity for lights and the trolley cars.

The streets were long and wide and crowded on both sides with bustling businesses and busy hotels. Rob walked into one of the latter, a large ornate hotel known as the Adams Hotel.

"Yes, sir," the clerk behind the desk said as Rob stepped up. "You'll be wantin' a room?"

"Yes," Rob said as he filled out the registration form.

"With a bath?"

Rob looked up in surprise. It had been a long time since he had enjoyed the pleasure of a private bathroom. "You have rooms with baths?" he asked.

"Absolutely, sir," the clerk answered proudly. "We've had guests from the East tell us that New York, Boston, Philadelphia and other such cities have nothing on us."

"Very good," Rob said. "In that case, I will take a room with a bath. Oh, and I would like to have this telegram sent. Would you tell me where the nearest office is?"

"If you wish, you may leave your message with me, and I will have it taken to the telegraph office."

For a moment Rob hesitated, then he smiled. Why not? After all, he wouldn't be able to keep the message secret from the operator anyway. Besides, Phoenix was certainly far enough away that there was little danger of his message falling into the wrong hands. He took the message he had written while still on the train and handed it to the clerk.

"Very well, have it sent at once, please, and give this hotel as the address for my answer."

"Right away, sir," the clerk said. The clerk handed a key to Rob. "Your room is on the third floor, in front," he said. "You have French doors which open onto a lovely balcony from which you can look out over the city."

"Thank you," Rob said.

Rob climbed the wide, carpeted stairs to the third floor, then found his room with very little difficulty. His room was equipped with a large bed, quite a change from the narrow bunk he was accustomed to using in the bunkhouse. There were also a sofa, table and chair, and a large wardrobe chest. In addition, there was a door that led to a small bathroom. But, miracle of all, his room was equipped with an overhead electric fan. He turned it on to see if it worked, and was rewarded by a cooling breeze from the spinning paddles. He was surprised by the modern conveniences of his room. He wasn't sure what he expected, but the thought of electric lights and fans out here seemed strange to him. Though Phoenix certainly did have all the marks of a bustling community, and as electricity was quite common in the East, he really saw no reason why a city the size of Phoenix would be denied.

The bathroom had a white and black checkerboard tile floor. The white porcelain bathtub stood upon claw feet, and the water spigots were silver and enamel. When Rob turned them, he was rewarded with a steady stream of water. He let the water run until the tub was nearly full, then he took off his clothes and settled gratefully into the refreshingly cool bath.

Nearly half an hour later Rob was clean and freshly dressed, standing on the balcony outside his room, watching the people below. The sounds of the city reached his ears, and he contrasted the noise of the city with the quiet of his ranch.

Rob smiled. It was *his* ranch, though in truth he had to force himself to think of it that way. He was so much a part of the cowboy scene now that even he sometimes regarded the ranch as being the property of some distant owner, and himself as but one of the pawns.

He wasn't a pawn, of course. He was the owner, and as such, he was the one who was being hurt by the improper administration of the ranch. Because of his disassociation with the ranch by distance, he had been totally unaware of any impropriety. It wasn't until he arrived at the ranch seeking adventure, that he learned of the improper management. The message he sent asked his lawyers in Boston to recommend a Phoenix lawyer to whom Rob could go with his problem. Rob watched the street for a while longer, then he went back into his room and lay on the bed to let the cool breeze from the spinning fan wash over his body. He had been on the train for quite a while, having left early in the morning. Perhaps a small nap would be in order before dinner

Rob was dreaming. In the dream he was holding a plank against the wall of the barn while Curly was driving nails. The sound of the hammer was deafening, overpowering everything in the dream until finally it woke Rob up. He could still hear the pounding. It was not until that moment that he realized the pounding he was hearing was not a dream, but was really a knock on the door.

"Just a minute," Rob called. He sat up and rubbed his head. He must have been more tired than he thought, for he had slept so soundly that for a moment he had a difficult time getting his bearings. Then the spinning fan made him remember where he was and why he was here.

There was another knock at the door.

"Mr. Barringer? Mr. Barringer are you in there?" a voice called from the other side of the door.

Rob stood up and walked over to the door, then opened it. A tall, gray-haired man stood in the corridor. He was well-dressed, and he smiled pleasantly.

"Are you Rob Barringer?" the man asked.

"Yes," Rob answered. He was confused. Who knew that he was here?

The man handed Rob a card. "My name is Peter Meyer, sir," he said. "I am a lawyer."

"A lawyer?"

"Yes," the man said. "You did wire your firm in Boston informing them that you were looking for a lawyer, did you not?"

"Uh, yes," Rob said. "Yes, I did."

"As soon as your firm heard from you, they wired me," Peter said. "You see, we have done quite a bit of business together in the past. In fact, I have even conducted some railroad business for your grandfather. Your grandfather is Andrew Barringer, is he not?"

"Yes," Rob said, and stepped back. "Won't you come in?"

"Thank you," Peter said. "That is most hospitable."

The two men walked over to the sitting area, where Rob sat on the sofa and Peter settled in the chair.

"I understand that you, yourself are a lawyer," Meyer said.

"While I have passed the bar, I've never practiced," Rob said.

"And why is that? The law is a noble profession."

"Oh, I quite agree. It's just that, for now, anyway, my interests lie elsewhere."

"That's quite understandable," Meyer said. "Now, Rob, what is it that I can do for you?"

"I think I am being systematically robbed," Rob said.

"Robbed? By whom?"

"By Les Garrison."

"Les Garrison? I've heard of him," Peter said. "Yes, he is the owner of the Turquoise Ranch, I believe."

"He isn't the owner," Rob said. "He is the manager"

"Yes, that's right," Peter said. "I believe I did know that. Wait a minute. Are *you* the owner?"

"I am," Rob said.

"I see. And you think he is robbing you, do you? Well, that's a common enough thing, I suppose. There are many ranches owned by absentee landlords, which are having a portion of the profit shaved off by unscrupulous managers. It's easy enough to cover, you know. They report excess losses, don't report herd growth, report sales of less than they actually make. Have you confronted Garrison with your suspicion?"

"No," Rob said.

"Well, Mr. Barringer, don't you think you should? After all, you should hear his side as well. You shouldn't just depend upon unsubstantiated rumor. From whom did you hear he was robbing you, anyway?"

"It's just little things I've picked up here and there," Rob said. "I've been working on the ranch."

"I beg your pardon?" Peter said with some surprise.

"I've been working on the ranch for nearly two months now," Rob said. "I, uh, am working there as a cowboy. No one knows my identity."

"What?" Peter asked. "Let me get this straight. You are employed by Turquoise Ranch as a cowhand, and no one there suspects you are actually the owner of the ranch?"

"That's right," Rob said. "At least, I don't think anyone knows."

"You'd better hope they don't find out," Peter said.

"Why? What do you mean by that?"

"Well, outside the fact that it would be dangerous if Garrison found out, I doubt that anyone else would take it too kindly either. They aren't the ones you'll have to worry about. You may lose a few friends. But if Garrison is guilty, and if he finds out you're spying on him, you could lose your life!"

"Listen, I want you to know that I didn't get started in this charade in order to spy on people," Rob protested.

"Oh? Then why did you start it?"

"I wanted to learn the business," Rob said.

"I'm sorry, friend, but that argument doesn't hold water. Being a cowboy is no way to learn how to run a ranch. There are men who have cowboyed for half a century, and they don't know the first thing about the business end of the deal."

"Maybe so," Rob said. He smiled. "The truth is I guess I was just looking for a little adventure and I thought concealing my identity would be the way to do it."

"Yes. Well, you may be letting yourself in for a little more adventure than you had planned on," Meyer said. "I guess we had better go about finding out if you're being cheated, and if you are, put the guilty party, or parties, in prison."

"No," Rob said quickly. "No, I don't want to put anyone in prison."

"Oh? And may I ask why not?"

"I'm not sure how many are involved," Rob said. "And there are some that I don't want to get hurt."

"Even if they're hurting you?"

"Even if they're hurting me."

"Anyone in particular that you are trying to protect?"

"No, I... that is, I'm not trying to protect him. I don't really think he is guilty. In fact, he's one of the first people I heard about the impropriety from."

"A common trick," Meyer said.

"What?"

"It's a common enough trick," Meyer repeated. "If this person, whoever he is, had the slightest suspicion that you might be more than just an ordinary cowboy, it would be smart to avert suspicion from himself by saying something to you. Who is it?"

"It's Jake Dunford, the foreman of the ranch."

"Jake Dunford? Not the one they call Big Jake?"

"Yes," Rob answered.

"What do you know of Big Jake?" Meyer asked.

"Not much," Rob admitted. "I think he came from Texas originally. I know he fought in the war, but that's about all I know. Everyone is pretty close-mouthed about their past. That's what has helped me to keep my own secret."

"Yes, well, in the case of Big Jake Dunford, he has every reason to keep quiet about his past. You know he's from Texas. Did you also know he was wanted there for murder and cattle rustling?"

"No," Rob said. "I've never heard that."

"I don't wonder," Peter said. "It isn't the sort of a past one likes to speak about."

"Are you sure?" Rob asked. "He doesn't seem like the type of man who would commit murder."

Peter laughed. "How many men have you known who have committed murder?"

"Well, none," Rob answered sheepishly.

"You're right about his having been in the war. But he didn't fight in the regular army. He rode with a group called McPike's Raiders. He and McPike, and the others like him, were out to get what they could from the war. They turned bad during the war, and didn't stop when it was all over. Dunford began rebuilding his herd from cattle that he claimed the carpetbaggers stole from him and other Texas Ranchers. Then I hear he shot it out with some deputies from the Cattlemen's Association. Four of them, it was, and he killed all four. After that he left the state and came to Arizona. Believe me, in this case, Texas' loss was not Arizona's gain. Do you think he's involved?"

"I hope not," Rob said. "For Melanie's sake, I sincerely hope not."

Peter rubbed his chin and looked at Rob for a moment. "Tell me, Mr. Barringer, would Melanie happen to be Dunford's daughter?"

"Yes," Rob admitted.

"Is she pretty?"

"She's beautiful," Rob said with more feeling than he realized.

"I see. So it isn't really Jake Dunford you are concerned about, it's his daughter. Are you courting her?"

"Mr. Meyer, I scarcely see that that is any of your business," Rob said rather harshly. "And for your information, I am aware of Mr. Dunford's war-time service." He recalled his conversation with Curley.

"Excuse my intrusion," Peter said. "But if I am to do my job adequately, I feel that I should have all the information available. I don't want to go out on a limb and then have that limb sawed off behind me because you happen to be in love with the guilty man's daughter."

"In the first place, I don't believe Big Jake is guilty, regardless of what you say about him," Rob said. "And in the second place, what I feel or don't feel about his daughter has no bearing on anything. As it so happens, Miss Dunford is engaged to Les Garrison, so I don't think it should enter into this at all."

"But it has entered into it," Peter said. He sighed. "Very well, you're the boss. If you don't want to put anyone in prison, we won't try. But if you don't want to put anyone in prison, just what the sam hill *do* you want me to do?"

"I want to find out if rustling is going on, and stop it."

"All right, maybe we can do that," Peter said. "With you working on the inside and me on the outside, it should be easy enough to accomplish. Now, what I will need from you is advance word about any large cattle transaction. If there is a big cattle buy or sale in the near future, you must let me know."

"How should I contact you?"

"Send me a letter," Meyer said. "Not to my office, that might arouse suspicion if anyone saw the address on the envelope. Here is my post office box number. Send it there." He wrote a number on a piece of paper and handed it to Rob.

"All right," Rob said, taking the paper.

"You know, Mr. Barringer, if you do find out and confront Garrison with the evidence, even if you don't have any plans to send him to prison, he may not take it kindly. You'll be killing the golden goose, if you get my meaning, and he may not like that. It could still be dangerous for you."

"Yes, I know."

"And despite the faith you have placed in Jake Dunford, you may be in just as much danger from him."

"I don't really think I'm in danger from Mr. Dunford."

"It's when you least suspect it, that you may be in the most danger."

"I'll be careful," Rob said.

"Good," Meyer said. He smiled broadly and stuck out his hand. "Then I shall look forward to doing business with you, sir, as I've enjoyed doing business with your grandfather in the past."

14

That evening, Rob, wearing a suit, white shirt, and tie, stepped into the Brown Dirt Cowboy Saloon for a beer. As he stood at the bar, nursing his beer, he thought of his discussion with Peter Meyer. Was he right? Was Jake Dunford actually wanted in Texas, for murder and cattle rustling? He hoped not. He liked Jake and wouldn't want to think he could actually be guilty of such a thing.

"No, please, leave me alone!" It was a woman's voice, and the tone made it clear that she was frightened.

"You come upstairs with me now, or I'll drag you upstairs," a man replied in a challenging voice.

"No, please, I don't want to go with you."

"You're a whore, it don't matter whether you want to go with me or not, as long as I'm payin'."

"No."

The man and woman were standing at the far end of the bar from Rob, and he looked toward them. By the way she was dressed, it was obvious to Rob that she was a bar girl... whether she was actually a prostitute or not, he had no way of knowing. The man accosting her was a short, bandy-legged man with a long, unkempt beard.

"I ain't a' goin' to tell you ag'in," the man said then he slapped the woman so hard that her knees buckled, and she had to grab onto the edge of the bar to keep from falling.

"Mister, leave the lady alone," Rob said.

The man looked toward Rob, and seeing how he was dressed, laughed.

"You'd better stay out of this, you fancy-dressed son of a bitch," the man said. "That is, 'lessen you're wantin' to get your ass shot."

"You don't seem to be holding a gun in your hand," Rob said.

"Ha! 'N you ain't neither."

"No, but I am holding a beer mug."

The man laughed, then turned toward a table where two other men were sitting. "Did you hear that? This fancy-pants dude is holdin' a beer mug."

"Oh, Moody, you better be a' scairt," one of the men at the table said.

Moody turned back toward Rob. "Just what is it you're a' plannin' on doin' with that beer mug, anyhow?"

"This," Rob said.

With the snap of his arm, Rob threw the beer mug toward Moody, hitting him right between the eyes. Moody dropped to the floor and Rob hurried over to him, pulled his gun from its holster, then handed it to the bartender who was looking on in shock.

"Hey, Mister, Moody's our friend!" one of the two men from the table shouted out.

"Then here, you take care of him," Rob said. He

picked Moody up, lifted him over his head, and threw him like a rag doll. Moody landed right in the middle of the table, smashing it flat and knocking over the two chairs in which the men were sitting.

There were exclamations of shock from the other patrons of the saloon.

"Why you son of a..." one of Moody's friends said, drawing his gun as he was getting up.

Rob reached him in two quick steps, and grabbing the man's wrist, squeezed it so hard that he dropped his pistol.

"Are you going to draw your gun, too?" Rob asked the third man.

"No," he said. "No, I ain't goin' to do nothin' like that."

"Why don't you three men just leave?" the bartender asked, and looking toward him, Rob saw that he was holding a shotgun.

The man who had just dropped his gun bent down to retrieve it.

"No," the bartender said. "I expect you'd better leave it here, Barney. Burleson, you pick up Barney's gun 'n bring it over here. Yours, too."

"Damn, Felix, you're takin' our guns?"

"You can come back for 'em tomorrow," the bartender said.

The other patrons laughed, and a few of them even applauded as the three men left the saloon.

"What do I owe you for the table?" Rob asked the bartender.

"Mister, you don't owe a damn thing," the bartender said. "The show you just put on was worth it."

"Thanks. I didn't finish my beer, so I'll be needing another," Rob said, reaching for his money.

"Your money ain't no good in here, Mister," a woman said. She was dressed like the young woman Moody had slapped, but she was obviously older.

"Comin' to the rescue of Rhoda Sue like you done, I'll be buyin' all you can drink tonight."

"Why, thank you, ma'am." Rob looked toward the young woman who had just been identified as Rhoda Sue. "Miss, are you all right?"

Rhoda Sue smiled, and put her hand to the bruise that was already beginning to form on her cheek.

"I'm... I'm fine, thanks to you."

"That's good to hear."

"Would you... uh... would you like to spend some time with me? It won't cost you nothin'."

It took Rob a second or two to realize what Rhoda Sue was suggesting then he smiled.

"I'll tell you what, why don't we spend some time together over dinner? My treat."

"No, I meant, uh..." Rhoda Sue was quiet for a moment, then she smiled, shyly. "Thank you that would be very nice."

APPROXIMATELY ONE HUNDRED and fifty miles north of Phoenix, Melanie and Les were having a conversation.

"Why do you ask?" Les responded to a question Melanie had just posed. He poured wine into Melanie's glass, then put the bottle back on the table. Melanie had eaten dinner with him earlier, and though the house-keeper had cleared away the table, they were still sitting over their wineglasses, talking.

"It just seems unusual that you would sell the cattle

for such a little amount. I happen to know that the going price is thirty-one dollars a head. You've just booked 3000 head for twenty-five dollars a head. That's fifteen thousand dollars less than we should be getting for them."

Les took a sip of his wine and looked at Melanie over the rim of his glass. He smiled.

"Maybe there are some things you would be better off not knowing," he suggested.

"Les, are you selling stolen cattle to those people?"

Les laughed out loud.

"Now where would I be apt to steal three thousand head of cattle from? That's almost an entire herd, my dear, as if you didn't know."

"I don't know where you would steal them. It's just that, well, when I mentioned it to Papa, he said anyone who would sell cattle that cheaply must be selling stolen cattle."

"Did you tell him I was?"

"No. I wanted to hear what you had to say first."

"That was smart of you. Melanie, there are things about this business that you don't understand. There are things that you are better off not understanding."

"Like what?"

Les poured another glass of wine for himself.

"Well, if you are better off not knowing, then I certainly shouldn't be the one to tell you, should I?"

"Les, I love Turquoise Ranch, and my father loves it as well. I hope you aren't doing anything that could hurt the ranch."

"You forget, Melanie, I *am* the ranch," Garrison said. "What happens on this ranch reflects directly on me. I'm not going to give all that up by doing something stupid."

"Are you telling me the truth?"

"Of course I am," Garrison said easily. "Now, my suggestion to you is that you quit worrying so much. Your father and I know what we're doing."

"My father? You mean my father is involved?"

Les laughed, a short, easy laugh. "Involved in what? I told you, there is nothing for him to be involved in, and nothing for you to be worrying about. The only thing I want you to be thinking about now, is our wedding. That will be soon, you know."

"Yes, I know. Just two more weeks."

"Oh, I meant to tell you, I would like to postpone it for an additional three weeks. I hope you don't mind."

"No, I don't mind," Melanie said. In fact, she wouldn't have minded postponing it forever, though she didn't say anything.

"Good, I thought you would go along with me on it. It's just that I know you will want your father at the wedding, and as he will be on the cattle drive, he wouldn't have a chance to be here unless it's postponed."

"Cattle drive? What cattle drive?"

"To Phoenix, my dear," Garrison said, smiling broadly. "The cattle we are talking about were just sold to the San Carlos Apache Indian Reservation which is quite near Phoenix, so we are going to have an old-fashioned cattle drive."

"That's foolish. Why would you do that, rather than loading them on a train?"

"It will give us more direct control over the cattle." Les smiled. "Besides, look at it as an adventure."

"A CATTLE DRIVE? You mean we're actually going to make an old-time cattle drive?" Curly asked in reply to Jake's announcement.

"That's right," Jake said. "There are three thousand head of cattle we have to deliver to an Indian reservation down near Phoenix."

"But why drive 'em, boss? They's railroad track running down to Phoenix."

"'Cause Les Garrison wants 'em driven," Big Jake said. "And as long as he's the manager of this ranch, I don't reckon we got much choice."

"Well, say, you ain't gonna get no complaint from me," Curly said. "It's been a while since I was on a genuine cattle drive. And won't ole Rob like it, though? He's gonna get him some real cowboyin' done, now."

"I guess we all are," Big Jake said.

"Are you gonna ramrod the drive, boss?" Curly asked.

"Yes," Jake said. He smiled. "That is, if I can remember what to do. It's been that long since I was on a drive, I'm likely to be as green as Rob."

"Ha," Ed, who was also present, put in. "You, the man what took a cattle herd right out from under Yankee eyes, 'n drove 'em for near nine hundred miles? You makin' out like you wouldn't know what to do? Who you tryin' to kid?"

Jake laughed. "I hope I'm not tryin' to kid myself," he said, "and I hope we can get enough drovers who are willing enough to follow me to make a drive."

"Don't you worry none about that, boss," Ed said. "You ain't gonna have no trouble gettin' men to follow you. I remember how it was durin' the war. They was men who would soak their britches in kerosene and follow you to hell, jus' to see you kick the devil in the ass."

"A lot of things have changed since the war," Jake said.

"Some things don't never change," Ed said. "And bein' a man others'll follow is one of those things. You're a leader, boss, natural born. Always was, and always will be."

Ed and Curly left to attend to various duties, while Jake thought of Ed's words. He had been a leader men would follow. But it hadn't always been good for his men. The ones who followed him during the war, and who survived, came home to find themselves wanted men. Those who followed him down the rustler's trail after the war found themselves riding down a one-way street to nowhere.

NEWS that the Turquoise outfit was going to drive three thousand head of cattle south in an old-time cattle drive spread quickly, and soon men began to show up looking for work. It was good that extra men showed up because a lot more men would be needed to drive the cattle a great distance than would be required merely to watch over them on the range. Some of the men who returned were men who had worked on Turquoise Ranch before and had left, cursing Les Garrison and swearing never to come back. But they, like the others, were attracted by the opportunity to participate in a genuine cattle drive, for this was now, mostly, a thing of the past.

"It will be something we can tell our grandchildren," the cowboys said to each other as they discussed the upcoming drive in the saloons and cafes of Flagstaff.

"Ha! Like any of us is ever' goin' to have any grandchildren," someone said.

There were many applicants for the drive, so many in

fact, that Big Jake had to put out a special table and sit behind it while he took the applications. The cowboys were lined up all the way across the yard.

"What's so unique about a cattle drive?" Rob asked Curly as the two men stood on the porch of the bunkhouse and watched the excited activity. "Isn't that normally the way you get your cattle to market?"

Curly laughed. "That was the way of it till the railroads come along. After that, they's been very few of 'em, 'n they's likely to be even fewer of 'em in the future. This here is gonna be just like the ole times, though, 'n that's why so many is showin' up."

"It must be good work."

"It's hard work," Curly said. "Most of these galoots don't have no idee what they're lettin' themselves in for. They jus' heard about it, 'n they're wantin' to get in on it. The others, the older ones that have been on a trail herd, are just wantin' to... to..." He let his voice trail off.

"To what?" Rob asked.

"I don't know as I can say it so's you can understand it. I ain't a educated man, 'n I can't talk fancy none like you can, but it's like they're all a' wantin' to reach out 'n take a' holt o' somethin' they think they had when they was young."

"They want to recapture their youth," Rob suggested.

"Yeah, maybe you could put it that way," Curly said. "The plain truth is, though, what most of 'em remember ain't what it's like a'tall. They jus' remember the good times, the days when they was plenty of water 'n lots of grass 'n no weather or animals or rustlers to spook the cows. They remember the friendly jawin' aroun' the campfires 'n the drinkin' and celebratin' at the end of the trail. They don't remember the bad parts."

"What are the bad parts?" Rob asked.

Curly looked at Rob, then Curly laughed and looked down at the ground in embarrassment.

"I don't know," he said. "I don't remember 'em neither, so I reckon the truth of it is, I'm just as big a fool as any of them are."

15

Melanie did not intend to let this opportunity pass. If there was going to be a cattle drive, she was going to go on it. She had heard her father and the other men talk about the cattle drives of old. They had told so many wonderful stories about them that the idea of an old cattle drive had taken on a magical quality. And now that there was to be one, she wasn't going to let the opportunity pass.

Melanie said nothing to Les about her plan to go on the drive. She knew that he would definitely be opposed to it. Actually, she felt that he really had no right to tell her whether or not she could go, since they weren't married yet, but she didn't want to argue with him about it, so she said nothing. Les Garrison wasn't the only person Melanie kept in the dark. She didn't talk to her father either. She just went to Ed and told him that she would be going with the trail herd as his assistant. She implied, though she didn't actually come right out and say it, that her father knew of her plans.

"I won't join you until midway the first day," she said.

"I have several things that need to be taken care of at home before I can leave."

"Whenever you join, it'll be fine," Ed said.

Melanie didn't really have a lot to do. She just felt that her chances of getting away with it would be much better if she pretended that she wasn't going to go.

On the day of the drive the cowboys who were going were up before dawn. Melanie could hear them from her bed as they called out and shouted excitedly and laughed and whistled at horses and each other. They banged around the barn and corral, loading wagons and preparing equipment for the drive. Ed was getting ready too, because Melanie could smell coffee and bacon from the cookhouse, and she knew that the cook had been up for hours already in order to prepare a breakfast for the men.

"Yo, Rob, take a look in that wagon and see if we packed away the spare harness," a voice called loudly. Melanie strained to hear Rob's answer, not because she was concerned as to whether the spare harness had been packed, but because she just wanted to hear Rob's voice. It came to her, clear and strong.

"It's all here."

The shouting and noise continued for another hour so that sleep was impossible, even for those who had no intention of going. Melanie didn't mind it, though, because she was enjoying the excitement, even from her bed. She wished she could get up and be a part of it, but she was afraid that if she did so, it would jeopardize her plans to go. She wondered how Les could be so insensitive to the excitement. Melanie knew that Les wasn't going. He was over in the Big House, still in bed. It was very unlikely that he would still be asleep though, as it would be nearly impossible to sleep through all the noise.

Finally, after a good hour of preparation, during which time the men ate breakfast in shifts, the wagons and the horses started to move out. Just as they started, Melanie heard a light tapping on her door.

"Melanie?" her father called. "Melanie, girl, are you awake?"

"Did you really think I could sleep through all this?" Melanie asked.

Jake laughed. "I guess not."

"Come on in, Papa," Melanie called back to him. She sat up in bed to watch him as he came into her room.

"I just wanted to tell you we were leavin' now," Jake said. "And I didn't want to leave without tellin' you goodbye."

"You're looking forward to this, aren't you, Papa?" Melanie asked. She laughed. "I've been watching you. You're enjoying it."

"I have to confess that the thought of doing another trail drive is appealin' to me," Jake said. "I only wish I could feel better about it."

"Better about it? What do you mean? Papa, you aren't expecting some sort of trouble, are you?" Melanie asked.

"No, darlin', nothing like that," Jake said.

"Then what is it?"

Jake looked at Melanie for a long moment, then he summoned up a smile. "Nothin', darlin'. At least, nothin' you've got to worry your pretty head about. Now, I've got some cows to move. You be a good girl and go on back to sleep."

Melanie smiled. "That's what you used to tell me when I was just a little girl."

"You're still my little girl as far as I'm concerned," Jake said.

Melanie lay back down after her father left her room, but she didn't go back to sleep. She was far too excited for that.

It was late morning by the time Melanie left the house. She had kept herself occupied with busywork, both to help pass the time until she could leave and, also, to fool Les into thinking everything was going along normally. She did a small wash and hung a few things out on the line, carefully choosing items that would dry quickly so she could take them in before she left. She waved gaily at Les when she saw him get in the buggy for a drive into town. She knew that he was going to town, and that was what she had developed her plan around. She would leave while he was gone. He was going to stay in town overnight so by the time he returned tomorrow, she would already be with the drive, and it would be too late for him to do anything.

Although the drive had been under way for three or four hours by the time Melanie left, she was able to cover the same ground on horseback in but one hour.

As she rode in the direction of the drive, it wasn't long before she could see a huge cloud of dust hanging just over the horizon.

She could sense the excitement, even before she was close enough to hear anything. She could also hear the sounds of the drive, the bawling and mooing of cattle and the shouts and whistles of the wranglers, before she could actually make anything out in the dust cloud. Finally, she could see the cows moving forward relentlessly, prodded on by the drovers. She rode around the edge of the herd, and headed for the chuck wagon. The chuck wagon, she knew, would be far ahead of the herd, perhaps nearly to the location of the first night's camp.

"Lunch is generally what a drover can carry with him," Ed had explained to Melanie when he was telling her about the drive. "Generally, it's no more 'n a piece of jerky and a swallow of water, ever' now 'n then maybe a handful of dried fruit. The only two meals the cowboys really get are breakfast and supper. Since them is the only two regular meals, I always do my best to make certain they are good ones. You see, what I do is, I fix 'em up a good breakfast, generally biscuits 'n gravy, or hotcakes, 'n lots o' hot, strong coffee. Then, after I've cleaned up, I break camp 'n go on ahead till I've gone whatever distance the trail boss tells me he plans to make that day. Then I make camp 'n start supper, beans, most likely, or chili, or a good stew. If I got enough time, 'n I have a good, large piece of beef, why sometimes I even whip up a barbecue. Whatever it is, I try 'n be prompt, 'cause come nighttime the herd is caught up to the chuck wagon, 'n the drovers is ready for their vittles. That means I got to have it hot 'n ready for 'em, 'cause they generally ain't in no mood to wait."

"I'll help all I can," Melanie said. "Whatever you want me to do, I'll do."

That conversation had taken place on the day Melanie told Ed she would be helping him. Now she was reviewing the conversation in her mind. If she was going to be successful in convincing her father to let her stay, she was first going to have to convince Ed that she was a help rather than a hindrance.

As Melanie passed the herd, she kept far enough around the edge of it so that no one saw her. Seeing the roundup in progress was much more exciting than listening to it from her room that morning. She could see the dark shapes of cattle moving under a billowing cloud of dust. She could see individual plumes of dust behind running horsemen as cowboys dashed hither and yon to keep the animals in check. She could hear the rattle of the cows' long horns, as they sometimes encountered one another. She wished she could take the time to stop and study the herd to see if she could pick out her father and Curly and Rob. But she knew that she would have to ride hard to catch the chuck wagon if she meant to join up with Ed in time to be of any assistance for supper. Because of that, she rode on ahead, spurring her animal into a long, ground-eating lope which she knew he could keep up for hours. Finally, she saw the wagon ahead, and she let out a little shout, then urged her horse into a gallop to catch up.

"You're just in time," Ed said when Melanie reached the wagon and swung down from her horse. Ed pointed to a sack of potatoes. "I'm gonna have a stew for supper I need those potatoes peeled."

Melanie smiled. It wasn't much of a greeting but she would rather be greeted with the prospect of some work to do, than to be told that she wasn't welcome. Willingly, she took the potatoes which were to be peeled and started to work.

Les Garrison had gone to Flagstaff to meet with Benjamin Broomfield and Richard Berry.

"Colorado Cattle Company will actually be receiving the money from the government in payment of the cattle. We've made all the necessary arrangements for the money, in the amount that we have agreed upon, to be paid to Jake Dunford," Broomfield said.

"Good, I've opened an account for Turquoise at the Valley National Bank in Phoenix, and have instructed Dunford to deposit the money there."

"You're depositing the money in an account for Turquoise?" Broomfield asked. "I thought you planned to open your own account."

Les smiled. "For all intents and purposes, it is my account. As I am setting up the account, I will do so in a way that grants me sole access."

"I'm just curious as to how you intend to keep this transaction a secret from the owner of the ranch," Broomfield said.

"I don't think there is an owner, per se'," Les said. "It may be a consortium of owners. I know that all my dealings are with Morgan, Trevathan, and Daigh, and they have been very good about giving me full autonomy."

"Morgan, Trevathan, and Daigh?"

"They are a legal firm in Boston. They may be the ones who actually own the ranch, I don't know. But I do know they are the ones I deal with."

Broomfield chuckled. "You do seem to have things under control," he said.

16

R ob couldn't recall when he had been so tired. It was a bone-aching, back-breaking tired, and yet there was an exhilaration, too, that transcended the tiredness. The exhilaration came from the excitement of the drive and from the feeling of accomplishing some good, hard work. Rob wasn't the only one affected by the excitement of the day. He could see it in the eyes and on the faces of all the other drovers as well. The excitement was infectious and self-feeding and it seemed to grow as the day progressed. It was all around them, like the smell of the air before a spring shower, or the smell of wood smoke on a crisp fall day.

But it wasn't fall or spring. It was summer, and throughout the long, hot day the sun beat relentlessly down on the men and animals below. Mercifully, the yellow glare of the early summer sky mellowed into the steel blue of late afternoon by the time the herd reached the place where it would be halted for the night and the cowboys were refreshed with a breath of cool air. To the west, the sun dropped all the way to the foothills, while to the east evening purple, like bunches of violets, gathered in the notches and timbered draws. Behind the setting sun, great bands of color spread out along the horizon. Those few clouds which dared to intrude on this perfect day were under lit by the sun and they glowed orange in the darkening sky.

Rob was watching the sunset with appreciation for its beauty when he heard Curly call to him.

"I'm over here, Curly," Rob called back.

Curly rode over to Rob, and the two of them looked toward the colorful display for a few, quiet moments.

"I've heard tell that the sunsets at sea are near 'bout as pretty as the ones we have out here," Curly said quietly, almost reverently. "But iffen you ask me, God'd be hard-pressed to make any sunsets better'n this here'n we're alookin' at."

"I've seen them at sea," Rob said. "And I agree with you, I've seen none more glorious than this."

Curly smiled. "Iffen someone would've asked me, I would'a told 'em you'd been to sea. I bet you been to Europe, too."

"Yes," Rob said.

"You're a queer one for a cowboy, Rob Barringer. But they can't no one say you ain't earnin' your keep. Speakin' o' which, you ain't through for the day."

"Oh? Why, did I fail to do something?"

"Naw, you didn't leave nothin' undone," Curly said. "But don't go thinkin' you can get all cozied up by the campfire 'n listen to the singin'. The boss has other plans for us."

"What sort of plans?"

"I figured the boss would go easy on you, bein' as this is your first drive 'n all, but what do you think? He's gone 'n tapped you 'n me for nighthawk."

"What do you mean, because this is my first drive?" Rob asked with a laugh. "It's just about everyone's first drive, isn't it?"

"Yeah," Curly replied. "Yeah, I guess it is at that. Well, come on. Bein' as we got to nighthawk, we at least get to go to the head of the grub line. And I'm that hungry tonight that I could eat mutton."

"Mutton? Oh, wouldn't a couple of lamb chops be good right now, though?" Rob asked. "Maybe with a little mint jelly and asparagus."

"What?" Curly said. "Are you serious? Are you really talkin' 'bout eatin' one o' them wooly bastards?"

"Of course, I'm serious," Rob said. "I think lamb is delicious."

Curly made a spitting noise, then shook his head. "Don't ever let a cowman hear you talk like that," he said. "I've known cowmen who would shoot a fella for such talk. You know, they's been many a range war fought between sheepmen and cowmen. Leastwise, iffen you are gonna carry on 'bout how good lamb is, you could have the decency to do it when I'm not aroun'. I wouldn't want to be hit by no stray bullets."

Rob laughed. "Thanks for the warning," Rob said. "I wonder what we will have. I'm a little hungry myself."

"Beans or stew," Curly said. "But either one is fine with me tonight."

Rob and Curly took their horses to the remuda and unsaddled them, because they would draw fresh mounts for their night duty. They dropped their saddles where they could retrieve them easily after supper, took their mess kits out of their saddlebags, and sauntered over to the chuck wagon to get their meal.

"Uhmm, stew, from the smell of it," Curly said. They saw Ed stirring something in a big, steaming cauldron, and then they saw Ed's helper, a small thin cowboy who was busy with something at the far end of the wagon. Because of the late evening shadows, neither Curly nor Rob could see the assistant very clearly.

"You want to know how to get a few extras during a drive?" Curly asked.

"Extras? What sort of extras?"

"I'm talking about things like an extra biscuit, or an extra piece of pie, things like that."

"Sure," Rob said, smiling. "I'm always willing to learn a few tricks of the trade."

"You got to make up to the cook's boy," he said. "The cooks nearly always got 'im some young boy helpin' out who really wants to cowboy, but helpin' the cook is as close as he can get. What you do is, you make friends with the boy, you know, let 'im ride your horse, show 'im a few things with a rope, stuff like that. Then you get to bein' sort of a hero to the boy, 'n the next thing you know, why, little extras start turnin' up in your plate." Curly pointed to the back of Ed's assistant. "Go on over there and get started."

"Oh, Curly, I don't know," Rob hesitated. "I'd feel a little foolish."

"What for?" Curly asked. "For someone who eats like you do, why, I would think you'd take any opportunity to get a little extra food. Besides which, you don't have to feel foolish just to be nice to a body, do you?"

"No, of course not."

"Then go on over there like I told you. You gonna need all the extras you can get, or you're likely to starve to death durin' this drive."

"All right," Rob said begrudgingly. Rob walked over to the slim assistant. "It certainly smells good around here," Rob said. "You must be doing a good job."

The assistant didn't answer, nor turn around. Rob looked back toward the head of the wagon where Curly was standing, holding his mess kit. Rob made a shrug with his shoulders, as if asking what he should do next, and Curly urged him on.

"I know you may think your job is unimportant," Rob said. "But believe me, it is every bit as important as mine, or any of the others. Why, without the knowledge that you and Ed were here working away to make certain that we had good, hot meals at breakfast and supper, I don't know if we could go on."

There was still no answer, so Rob cleared his throat and started again.

"Of course, I know you may not feel that way sometimes. When a boy has his heart set on riding herd, I guess it might be a little disappointing to be stuck on chuck wagon detail. But look, I'll tell you what I'll do. Anytime you would like to ride my horse, why you just come look me up and I'll be glad to oblige."

"Thanks," the assistant said, without turning around.

Rob was confused by the lack of response from the boy, and he wondered if he should say more. Then, fortunately Curly called to him.

"Come on, Rob, iffen we're gonna get re-mounts and back to the herd, we gotta eat now."

"Right," Rob said. He shrugged his shoulders and walked back to join Curly at the steaming cauldron.

"How'd you make out?" Curly asked.

"That's a quiet young man," Rob said. "I could hardly get a word out of him."

"Who?" Ed asked as he spooned a generous portion of stew into Rob's kit.

"The boy you got belly-robbin' for you," Curly said.

"Me 'n Rob figured to make friends with him, but he didn't seem none too friendly."

Ed smiled broadly. "Tryin' to get inside for a little extra grub, are you?"

"Now Ed, you know me," Curly said.

"You mighty damned right I know you," Ed said. "That's why I said what I said. You don't think I'm some calf just birthed yesterday, do you? I been aroun' awhile. I know all the tricks you might come up with."

"Yeah? Well, it didn't work anyway," Curly said. "You done picked yourself one unsociable boy as your assistant."

"Well, now that's funny," Ed said, smiling again. "'Cause I think my assistant is just about as sociable as they come."

"Is that so? Well, why don't you call him over here so we can get better acquainted," Curly suggested.

Ed smiled again and shouted to his assistant, "Come on over here and meet these two galoots who think you're so unsociable."

Ed's assistant sauntered over, then, at the front of the wagon, removed a hat which let a cascade of long strawberry blonde hair tumble down. Melanie laughed.

"Miss Melanie!" Curly gasped. "It's you?"

"One and the same," Melanie said.

Now it was Curly's time to laugh. "Well, I gotta say, you put one over on us, didn't she, pardner?"

"Yeah," Rob said. "So it would seem."

A COOL NIGHT breeze swept over Rob. It was not a strong breeze at all, for the nearby trees did no more than whisper with its passing, but its breath was pleasant against Rob's skin. In the distance a coyote barked, and he was answered by the long, plaintive howl of another.

Above Rob the white stars blazed bright, big and close. Before him, a large shuffling shadow within shadows, the herd stood, content for the moment with resting for the night. Behind him, a distance of nearly a mile, campfires winked tiny orange lights as the cowboys gathered around for their supper and evening discourse. Rob and Curly had already had their supper, and any discourse they would have now would have to be in the quiet shadows of the herd as they rode on their lonely night vigil.

Abruptly, Rob jerked his head around at the sound of iron striking stone. It came from Curly's horse as he rode up toward him.

"I've circled the entire herd," Curly said. "They was a handful on the other side that was gettin' a bit antsy, but I pushed 'em on back into the herd. I figger they'll stay with the others, but we might want to take a look ever' now 'n ag'in."

"All right," Rob said.

The two men rode on slowly. The cattle lowed softly and the crickets chirped noisily. By a quirk of the evening breeze a cowboy's laughter carried to them.

***

THE POTS and pans were clean and the "necessaries" drawer straightened out, so at last Melanie's long day was finished. She hadn't even rolled out her bedroll yet, and it was late at night, and many of the cowboys had already fallen asleep, exhausted from the day's work.

"Melanie?"

"Oh, Papa," Melanie said, turning toward the sound of the voice. "I didn't know you were here."

"That makes us even. I didn't know you were here, either. What are you doing here?"

"I wanted to come."

"You might have asked me if you *could* come."

"Would you have let me?"

"I don't know. No, I don't think so."

"Well then, so much for asking you."

"I wish you hadn't come. A trail drive is no place for a woman."

"Papa, haven't you told me the story many times of Mom going on the drive up to Denver with you?"

"That was different. She had me to look after her."

"How is it different? I have you to look after me, too."

"It's not the same thing."

"Oh? Would you feel more secure about me if Les were on the drive, looking out for me?"

"No, it isn't that. It's just that... well, this isn't an ordinary drive, darlin'. There's somethin' strange about this drive, 'n I'm not sure I like the smell of it."

"I know. You suggested that once before. But when I asked you if you expected trouble, you said no."

"Well, I don't expect trouble. That is, not the kind of trouble you think of when you think of trouble on a trail drive. But there's trouble and then there's *trouble*. And if it comes, I'd just as soon you not be around."

"Papa, you aren't going to send me back now, are you? Ed is counting on me. He thought I was coming along, so he didn't bother to hire anyone to help him. It's either me, or you'll have to pull someone off the drive. Have you got enough men to do that?"

"No, and you know I don't." Big Jake sighed and ran

his hand through his hair. "Melanie, I don't like bein' put on a spot like this."

"I know you don't, Papa, and I hated to do it. But I wanted to go on this drive and I knew that if I asked you, you would probably say no."

"You're right. I would have. I can't understand Les letting you come."

"Les didn't let me come," Melanie said.

"What do you mean?"

"I just came. Les doesn't know anything about it."

Jake laughed. "You mean Les doesn't even know you left?"

"No, and I doubt if he'll find out before tomorrow. He went into Flagstaff, and I think he plans to spend the night there."

Jake laughed again. "In that case, darlin', stay with the drive. Stay with the drive and Les be damned!"

It was with some confusion that Melanie lay out her sleeping roll that night. She was glad that her father had consented to her staying with the drive, but confused by his strange reaction to the knowledge that her presence was secret from Les. Her father had never been openly hostile toward her association with or engagement to Les Garrison, but he had never been warm to it either. Tonight, he had come the closest he had ever come to letting his true feelings be known. It was now obvious that her father did not like Les.

The question was, why not?

After all, Les was everything a girl could want in a man. He was handsome, almost to a fault. He was ambitious, and his ambitions had already borne fruit, for he was the manager of one of the largest and most productive ranches in the territory of Arizona. It would seem to

Melanie that any father would be more than pleased to have a daughter in love with such a man.

In love with?

At that thought, Melanie's musings stopped. She was engaged to Les, and she was going to marry him. But was she in love with him?

Of course, she was in love with him. Why else would she have agreed to marry him? Any doubts she might feel now were caused by her strange reactions to Rob Barringer. Why?

Rob Barringer wasn't handsome.

Rob Barringer wasn't wealthy.

Rob Barringer wasn't even ambitious, or he would certainly not be working as a mere cowboy.

In fact, Rob Barringer might even be fleeing some social or civil indiscretion that had occurred back East. So what was there about him that held such a strange attraction for her? It was foolish. It was beyond foolish, and she was determined to put him out of her mind.

There, see how easy that was? she asked herself. *I'm not even thinking about him now.*

Melanie chuckled. "Yeah, right," she said aloud.

17

After Jake left Melanie, he walked through the sleeping men, beyond the chuck wagon, even beyond the remuda, before he found a rock that was just about the right size for sitting. He sat on the rock, pulled the makings from his pocket and rolled a cigarette. He lit up, then, savoring the satisfying taste of a good smoke, he thought of Melanie's remark about her mother.

Melanie reminded Jake of Maggie. Melanie looked so much like her that sometimes, in the shadow of an afternoon or in a certain trick of light, a sharp pain would come to his heart, because he could almost believe that Melanie was Maggie come back to him.

They were more alike than mere lookalikes, though. They were alike in spirit and personality.

Maggie's last thoughts had been of him, and their then, ten-year-old daughter.

"Jake," she said, her voice strained from the effects of meningitis. "Take care of our daughter, and know that, every time you look at her, you'll be seeing a part of me."

"JAKE? JAKE, IS THAT YOU?" Ed called. Ed's voice brought Jake back from his memories, and he looked around to see his friend walking toward him.

"Yeah," Jake said. "It's me."

"I thought I saw you walking over here. You got a smoke?"

Jake took the makings from his pocket and handed them to Ed.

"I hope you don't mind too much my lettin' the girl come along," Ed said. "But the truth is I'd rather have her along with us than back there with Garrison."

"It won't be long, Ed, till she's with Garrison all the time. She's goin' to marry him, you know."

"I keep hopin' somethin' will come up to prevent that," Ed said. He put the rolled cigarette in his mouth and lit it. "'Cause iffen it don't, I'm just likely to prevent it myself."

Jake chuckled. "And how would you do that?"

"Oh, easy. I'd shoot the son of a bitch."

"That might not be a bad idea," Jake said, with another chuckle. "But the truth is, Ed, all we can do is stand by and watch. Melanie is a full-grown woman now. She's got the right to make up her own mind to make up, 'n has her own life to live. If she decides she wants to live it with Les Garrison, I don't really reckon there's much we can do about it."

"Garrison's stealin' Turquoise blind, you know," Ed said.

Jake sighed. "Yeah, I know."

"He's real slick with it," Ed said. "But he's gonna get caught, 'n when he does, the owners are gonna come down on him like a duck on a June bug. But, 'n here's the thing, Jake. There ain't no way you're gonna escape that either."

"I know that, too," Jake said.

"Seems to me like the best thing to do would be just to take Garrison outa the picture."

"You mean kill him? I thought you were just teasing."

"Killin' ain't no stranger to either one of us, Jake."

"I know. But neither of us have ever killed except during the war, or when we have actually been challenged in a gun battle. We've never taken it upon ourselves to play God."

"I know. That's why I figure to just prod the son of a bitch till he draws on me," Ed said. "Hell, I might even give the son of a bitch the first shot. Then I'll kill him."

"He's too slick for that," Jake said. "And I don't know that I want him dead. I'd rather let him live and let Melanie see him for what he is."

"Do you reckon she will?"

"She's a real smart girl, Ed, she'll come to her senses. I just know she will."

AT THAT VERY MOMENT, Les Garrison, the subject of their conversation, was spending the night in Flagstaff just as Melanie had known he would. What Melanie did not know was that he was not spending it alone. He was with Mattie Tyre, a soiled dove whose company he had enjoyed before.

Mattie led Les up the back stairs of Cahill's, and down a long, narrow hallway to the room that was hers. She lit a lantern as soon as she was inside, and the room was bathed in a quivering bubble of golden light. She smiled at Les and pointed to the table.

"You know where it is, love," she said. "You've been here often enough."

"Yeah," Garrison said. "I know where it is."

Les reached for the whiskey and two glasses. He pulled the cork with his teeth and splashed the liquor into the glasses.

"Les, is it true you're going to marry the daughter of your ranch foreman?"

"Where did you hear that?" Les asked.

"I heard it," Mattie said. "I heard it from the woman she bought material from to make a wedding dress. Is it true?"

"What if it is?" Les asked.

"You… you promised to marry me," Mattie said in a quiet, hurt voice.

Les turned toward her and laughed, a laugh without mirth.

"You?" he said. "Did you honestly think I would marry you?"

"You told me you would," Mattie said.

"That was just talk, you shouldn't have believed me."

"Why not?"

"Because they were lies, told in a whore's bed," Garrison said cruelly. "You've been a whore long enough now—you should be able to recognize them."

"I … I thought you were different," Mattie said. "I thought I meant something to you."

Les held his hand out toward the bed. "This is all you meant to me," he said. "And this is all you'll ever mean." He smiled. "But don't be sad. I'll still come to see you, even after I'm married. Nothing need change between us."

"You mean… you want to see me even after you're married?"

"Sure, why not?"

Shutters seemed to descend in Mattie's eyes, and the windows that had opened to her soul suddenly closed. For a few moments, she had been vulnerable. But no more. Now she moved behind those shutters and covered herself up so that she could never be hurt again.

"Sure," she repeated. "Why not? Only it will cost you more."

"It will cost me more? Why?"

"I charge more when I have to go to bed with someone who is a son of a bitch," Mattie said flatly.

Les laughed. "Indeed," he said.

———

THERE WERE VERY few left at the ranch when Garrison returned. He stabled his horse then stepped into the Big House.

"Rosita," he called out to the Mexican woman who cooked, and kept house for him. "I'll be inviting Miss Dunford over to have dinner with me, so cook a little extra."

"Si, Senor," Rosita replied.

Garrison walked over to the house of the ranch foreman, stepped up on the porch, and knocked on the door.

"Melanie?" he called.

When he got no answer, he knocked and called out again.

"Melanie?"

When he wasn't answered this time, he tried the door, and finding it locked, used his key to let himself in. Neither Jake nor Melanie knew that Garrison had a key to their house, but Garrison figured that as the ranch manager, it was his right to have a key to any building on the ranch.

"Melanie?" he called again as he stepped inside. It took less than a couple of minutes to explore every room in the house, to discover that it was empty.

Puzzled by his inability to find her, Garrison went to the stable. Both the buggy and the buckboard were there, and if she had gone into town, she would have more than likely taken the buggy or the buckboard. And anyway, if she had gone into Flagstaff, Garrison would have, for sure, seen her.

Puzzled by her absence, he checked the stalls, and saw that her horse was gone. He didn't think she would have ridden her horse into town, her only reason for ever going into town was to do some shopping, and if she had gone shopping, it was very unlikely she would have used her horse to bring back any purchases.

Where was she?

As Cason contemplated the mystery of her absence, he realized that he was actually angrier, than he was concerned. This would not happen once they were married. She would have a role to play, and unannounced disappearances would not comport with what he had planned for her. He would make certain that she understood that.

Les was due to make a great deal of money from this operation. Even though this would be the single biggest score he had made, he had also made money from previous acts of larceny committed against Turquoise Ranch. It was his intention to reach the goal of one hundred thousand dollars. When he did so, he would leave Turquoise Ranch, and buy a ranch of his own. And he knew just what ranch that would be. Trailback Ranch was nearly as large as Turquoise, and there were several places where the two ranches shared a common property line, to say nothing of the free range that both ranches used.

Once he established himself as a property owner, and a man of means, he intended to investigate further pursuits, maybe even so far as getting himself appointed as governor of the Arizona Territory. And why not? Fremont was appointed governor with far less qualifications that he had.

18

The cattle drive continued without incident except for the long, tiring days in the saddle, and nights that were too short and too hot to allow the weary cowboys much sleep.

Melanie worked just as hard as any of the cowboys, and Ed paid her the supreme compliment of telling her that he had never been blessed with an assistant who was as good a worker as she was. But Ed didn't just tell Melanie, he told her father as well, and that made Melanie very glad about having come, for she knew that she was carrying her own weight. She commented on it.

"Oh, I'd say you're more than carrying your own weight," Ed said. He chuckled. "Your pa knows it, too, or he would have probably sent you back by now. He won't tolerate laziness, 'n I don't reckon he'd put up with it in his own daughter any more'n he would in anyone else."

"Ed, you've known Papa a long time, haven't you?"

"I reckon I've known him awhile. We was friends even before the war."

"Papa never talks about the war," Melanie said.

"It ain't a chapter in our history that folks need to be proud of," Ed said. "Neighbor fought ag'in neighbor, brother ag'in brother. 'Twas little honor in that war, girl."

"Were you a cook during the war?"

Ed chuckled. "Darlin', I was a little bit of ever'thin', and so were we all. We was irregulars, 'n we was behind the enemy lines most o' the time."

"What did you do behind the enemy lines?"

Ed chuckled. "We did things that would o' got us put in prison for sure durin' peacetime. We robbed a few Yankee banks, but we didn't keep any of the money. We give it all to the Confederacy. Only, when we come home, we discovered that the Yankees had done the same to us, 'n they weren't ready to give it back. So we took it back. We also rustled some of our own cattle back from the Yankees."

"You... you rustled cattle?" Melanie asked.

"That we did, girl. But you gotta understand, it was rightfully ours in the first place, even if the law didn't see it like that."

"Is Papa still rustling cattle?" Melanie asked quietly.

Ed looked at Melanie with a sharp expression on his face.

"Where did you hear that?" he asked.

"I didn't hear it anywhere," Melanie said. "It's just something I want to know."

"Look here, girl, you'd best be askin' your Papa some o' these questions," Ed said. "It ain't my place to be answerin' for him."

"I was just wondering, that's all," Melanie said.

"Well, quit your wonderin' 'n make yourself useful. Here, go get some water," Ed said to change the subject.

Melanie didn't ask any more after that, because she didn't want to upset Ed. And in truth, though she didn't admit it even to herself, she wasn't sure she wanted to hear the answers that Ed might decide to give.

In the meantime, she was genuinely enjoying the drive despite the hard work and the long hours. In fact, there was only one troublesome note, and that was Rob Barringer.

Melanie had to see Rob every day. She couldn't avoid him; he came through the grub line twice a day. She decided to change her tactics. Instead of being cold to him as she had been at first, she started going out of her way to be pleasant.

When Melanie first changed her attitude toward him, Rob was a bit wary of her conduct.

But Melanie's persistence paid off, and Rob was finally convinced that she was genuinely changing her attitude toward him. Once that was established he was able, like any of the other cowboys, to banter about and tease her.

But the banter and teasing was bittersweet for both of them. Melanie was able to see Rob's great sense of humor and fair play, and that, added to all his other qualities, made him all the more likeable. And Rob saw a new side of Melanie, a warm, tender side to go along with her beauty and vivaciousness.

Because of this bitter sweetness, it had almost been easier on them when they could fool themselves into thinking that they didn't like each other. Now they knew what a lie that was, and though neither one of them would admit it, they were strongly attracted to each other.

One night, a week into the drive, Melanie lay on her bedroll trying to go to sleep. A campfire burned cheerily in the center of the cowboy's circle, about thirty yards away. Most of the cowboys were already asleep because morning came early and the chance to rest was rarely squandered. A few cowboys were still awake, though, and Melanie could see them moving around as their shadows crossed back and forth in front of the flickering flames.

"Hey, Smiley, I thought you had nighthawk," one of the cowboys called to another.

"Naw," Smiley answered. "Rob's got it. I had it last night."

"Well, come on over here, Bob's telling us 'bout the girls he's gonna fix us up with in Phoenix."

"Ha, I can just see the girls he can get for us."

Smiley joined the others and then their conversation grew so quiet that Melanie couldn't hear it, though she could hear the occasional bursts of laughter which came from the men.

Melanie turned and positioned herself a dozen times, but no matter what she did, sleep refused to come to her on this night. Finally, she decided to get up and take a walk with the hope that the night air would soon make her sleepy. She found herself walking toward the remuda, and almost before she realized what she was doing, she saddled a horse. Moments later she was riding out toward the herd.

After a short ride, Melanie was completely away from the camp, swallowed up by the blue velvet of night. The night air caressed her skin like fine silk, and it carried on its breath the scent of pear cactus flowers. Overhead the stars glistened like diamonds and in the distance mountain peaks rose in great and mysterious dark slabs against the midnight sky. Melanie was aware of the quiet herd, with cows standing motionless in rest. An owl landed nearby and his wings made a soft *whirr* as he flew by. He looked at her with great round, glowing eyes, as if he had been made curious by her presence.

Melanie rode quietly for several moments until she came to a small grass-covered knoll. Here, she heard a splashing, bubbling sound, and she knew that she was hearing the swift flowing mountain stream which had caused them to choose this as the camping spot for the night. The stream provided water for men and cattle. Melanie had seen it when they first arrived, for she had gotten water for cooking from it. In fact, the chuck wagon was parked beside it. But that was at another location. Melanie had not seen the stream here.

Melanie got off her horse and walked to the top of the grassy knoll to look at the water. Here the stream was fairly wide and strewn with rocks. The water bubbled white as it tumbled over and rushed past the glistening rocks. The white feathers in the water glowed brightly in the moonlight while the water itself winked blackly, and the result was an exceptionally vivid contrast which made the stream even more beautiful at night than it was by day.

Melanie felt drawn to the water, and she walked all the way down the knoll until she found a soft wide spot in the grass. She sat down and pulled her knees up under her chin and looked at the water. The constant chatter of the brook soothed her, and she sat there in contemplative silence.

"I thought it was you I saw ride over this way. At least, I hoped it was you."

Melanie was startled by the sudden intrusion, and she turned to see Rob standing at the top of the knoll behind her.

"Aren't you supposed to be watching the herd?" Melanie asked.

"They're quiet," Rob said. "What are you doing out here so late?" He walked down the little hill and, uninvited, sat beside her.

"I couldn't sleep," Melanie said.

"As hard as you've been working and as early as you have to get up, I can't imagine you having trouble sleeping."

"I guess I just have too much on my mind."

"Are you thinking about your wedding?"

In fact, Melanie had been thinking about her father, and wondering whether or not he was involved in dishonest dealings with the owner of the ranch. But she didn't want to tell Rob that, so she let him think that he had guessed the truth.

"Yes," she said. "I was thinking about the wedding." There was very little enthusiasm in her reply.

"You don't sound very excited about it," Rob said.

"I'm going to marry him," Melanie repeated, with as little enthusiasm as before.

"Melanie, I, uh, well, I have no right to say this, I mean you're going to be the wife of the manager of the ranch, and I'm just a common cowboy."

"Rob Barringer, whatever you are," Melanie said with a little laugh, "you are no *common* cowboy."

"If you weren't engaged to marry Garrison, I wonder if . . ."

"You wonder if what?"

"I wonder if there might be an opportunity for the two of us to explore a more meaningful relationship."

"Oh, Rob," Melanie said. "Please, don't make this any harder than it is."

"I'm sorry," Rob said. "I've no want to cause you any discomfort. I spoke out of place."

"It's not as much out of place, as it is out of time,"

Melanie replied. "Like I said, I'll be marrying Les Garrison."

"Do you love him?"

"Rob, like I said, please don't make this any harder than it is."

"I'm sorry."

"It's just that, there are some things you don't know, some things that are . . ."

"Extenuating circumstances," Rob added.

"Yes, you might say that."

"Who knows, maybe things will work out better than you think."

"I don't know how you think that they can."

Rob smiled. "Let's just say that I am the consummate optimist."

"You are . . ." Melanie let the sentence hang.

"I'm what?"

"You are the most unusual person I've ever met. You are an educated man, but here you are, working as a cowboy. What did you actually study in school? Did you finish college?"

"Oh, yes, I have a *juris* doctor degree."

"A *juris* doctor? What kind of degree is that?"

"It's a law degree."

"My goodness, you mean you are a lawyer?" Melanie said, shocked by the pronouncement.

"Well, technically no, I'm not a lawyer, in that I'm not practicing law."

Melanie chuckled. "No, you're herding cattle."

"So I am."

"But why? I mean, if you are... Rob, are you in some sort of trouble? Have you come out here to get away from the law? No, wait, don't answer that question. It's none of my business."

"But of course, it's your business," Rob said. "It's the business of anyone with whom I associate. But to set your mind at ease, no, I'm in no sort of legal trouble."

"I'm glad."

Rob chuckled. "Yeah, I'm glad too."

19

Though Melanie didn't tell anyone of her visit with Rob, she couldn't help but think about it. For some reason his suggestion that things might work out better, and his declaration of being an optimist, sparked her own optimism.

Could things work out better? And what exactly would that mean?

She wanted so much to discuss what she was feeling, but who could she talk to? Ed? After all, since her horse had been turned in to the remuda, they rode together day in and day out, sitting side by side on the seat of the chuck wagon. No, she couldn't talk to him. She mustn't.

They worked together getting the meals prepared, and though it had been Melanie's habit to break into spontaneous song or make jokes or mention the glory of the sunset, or the majesty of the mountains, she was uncommonly quiet now, and Ed knew that something was different. Finally, when he could take it no longer, he asked Melanie what was wrong.

"What do you mean?" Melanie answered. She was

mixing dough for biscuits, and she had flour up to her elbow and a bit on the end of her nose. "What makes you think something is wrong?"

"Because," Ed said, "if there is anybody in this world who knows you as well as your pa, it's me. I've known you from the day you was borned, and I know something has happened, and whatever it was, it has happened just since this drive began."

"Ed," Melanie started, then paused for a long time, then sighed. "I think I'm in love."

"In love, are you? Well, seein' as you're a' gonna marry up with 'im, I guess it's prob'ly a good thing you're in love with 'im."

"But, oh, Ed, what I'm feeling can't be. It just isn't right."

"Well, I can sure agree with you there. But it ain't my place to say nothin'."

"Say it, Ed. You're part of the family."

"You're makin' a mistake."

"Why do you say that?" Melanie asked anxiously. "Do you know something I don't know?"

"All I know is that Les Garrison is a low-down excuse for a man, and I wouldn't..."

"Oh," Melanie said with a sigh of relief. "It's not Les Garrison I'm talking about."

"What? Look here, girl, when you tell me you're in love, you're not talkin' about Les Garrison?"

"It's not Les Garrison," Melanie said.

"But you're goin' to marry him?"

"No, I don't think I will marry him."

"Does your pa know this, girl?"

"No, Pa doesn't know this, nobody knows, not even the one I think I'm in love with. It's a secret from everyone."

"Who is it? Tell me."

"No, it would be best if I say nothing more about it," Melanie said.

"Girl, it would've been better if you'd never said anything about it in the first place. You know you're gonna tell me."

"I don't know, I just don't think I should."

Ed looked directly at her. "Who in tarnation are you in love with?"

"You have to promise that you won't say a thing about it to anyone, especially not him, and that you won't tell Papa."

"Why do I have to promise that? Your pa is the best friend I have in the world. Don't you think your pa has a right to know?"

"Of course, he should know, but I think I'm the one who should tell him, that is, when I know I have something to tell him. I've always suspected he wasn't happy about my engagement to Les anyway."

"Ha!" Ed said. "You sure got that right. Fact is, he's been miserable over your engagement to that no-'count, Now, *who* is it you've fallen for?"

"You haven't promised."

"All right, all right, I promise!" Ed said, holding up his right hand in the approximation of an oath. "Now, who is it?"

"It's Rob Barringer," Melanie said.

Ed smiled broadly and slapped his hand against his thigh.

"Ha!" he said. "I know'd it. I know'd it all along, that it was Rob."

"Oh? And how did you know?"

"I could tell by the way that you was shootin' moon eyes at him."

"Moon eyes?"

"Yeah," Ed said. "Just like the ones your mama used to give to your pa."

"Did Mama look at Pa like that?"

"That she did, girl, that she did."

"Tell me about Mama."

"Tell you about your mama? Shucks, girl, what can I tell you about your mama? You remember her well enough."

"No, I don't mean the mother that a young girl knew. I mean the one before. Before I was born. Before she and Papa were married. Tell me about her then. Was she as pretty then as I remember?"

Ed smiled and got a faraway look in his eyes.

"Girl, your mama was that pretty that she could pure take a man's breath away. She had eyes the color of a frosty morning sky and hair as golden as ripe wheat. Beautiful? I'll say she was beautiful."

"Did Papa really rescue her on the very first day he ever saw her?"

"That he did. Two desperadoes waylaid your mama and your gran'pa. Your gran'pa, you see, had brought in some cattle to sell. That's when Dolan and Phillips, two no-'counts jumped him. They knew about the cattle sale, and they was aimin' to take all the money."

"And Papa stopped them?"

"Yes, ma'am. Your pa always was that slick with a pistol that he could'a earned his keep as a gun for hire iffen he'd a had a mind to. Anyway, your pa braced them two men, 'n they was dumb enough to go up ag'in him. He shot 'em through, dead center, 'n cut 'em both down slick as a whistle. What that done was, it saved your mama and your gran'pa's lives."

"Tell me about Mama and Papa's courtship," Melanie said.

Ed smiled again. "Well, I reckon you could say that it started that very day."

"Really?"

"As far as your pa was concerned, it did," Ed said.

"What makes you say that?"

"Well, sir, when we told 'im that we were looking for Curly Stevens and the Turquoise Ranch, that's when we learned that your grandpa was foreman of the Turquoise, and he hired both of us.

"That night, me 'n your pa slept in the Turquoise bunkhouse, 'n that was the first time we'd had a roof over our heads in over two months. Well sir, we lay there 'n talked about our good luck at landin' us a job so quick. And that was when your pa told me he was gonna marry your mama."

"You mean he'd already asked her?" Melanie asked in surprise.

"Asked her? No, not a word of it. But that didn't make no never mind to your pa. He had it in his mind he was gonna marry her, 'n that was that."

"Tell me about Mama."

"Well, like I said, she was as pretty as a new-foaled colt. That part you already know. But did you know that they wasn't a soul in the territory that could touch her on horseback, and that's man or woman. She could ride like the wind."

"You mean she could have beaten Papa?"

"Oh, girl, your pa couldn't even come close to her."

"That must have been embarrassing to Papa."

"No. Your ma was that good that it didn't embarrass anyone to be beat by her." Ed chuckled. "Besides, your gran'pa always used to say that he never doubted for a moment that your mama wanted to be caught by your pa, 'cause they couldn't nobody catch that girl, without she was wantin' to be caught."

"Did Grandpa approve of Pa? Was he pleased that they got together?"

"Yes, I'd say your gran'pa was pleased. He always set a great store by your pa, and he stuck by him, even when there was trouble."

"What trouble?" Melanie asked.

"You got to remember that after the war there was quite a bit of paper out on your pa 'n me back in Texas. It was only natural with as many folks arriving in Arizona from Texas as there was durin' those days that someone was goin' to come who would remember us."

"And did they?"

"Worse. Some bounty hunters came out, bound to make a little money on takin' our scalps back to Texas. The fact is, that by then all the warrants had been erased, and the paper was supposed to be all called back. Me 'n your pa wasn't wanted men no more. But bounty hunters are men with cow plop for brains. They had them a piece of paper that had a dead-or-alive reward on it, and that was all they cared about. They came lookin' for us, aimin' to turn our killin' into a little money in their pockets."

"What happened?"

"It was just before your mama and your pa got married. About a week before, I think it was. Me, your pa 'n your gran'pa had gone into town. Your gran'pa was at the bank, your pa was runnin' errands for your mama, 'n I went into the Gilded Cage."

Melanie laughed.

"The Gilded Cage, Ed? Really ... The Gilded Cage?"

"It was a bar and..."

"Sporting house?" Melanie teased.

"Watch your tongue, girl. You aren't supposed to know about such things."

"It was a sporting house, wasn't it? It was a place where soiled doves live and work."

"Girl, iffen your pa knew me 'n you was talkin' about such a place, he'd have my hide!"

"Tell me about it. Did it have red lace curtains and lots of gilt-edged mirrors?"

"Now, do you want me to tell the story or don't you?" Ed asked.

"I'm sorry," Melanie laughed. "Yes, I want you to tell the story. Please, do go on."

"All right. There I was, in the…"

"Sporting house," Melanie injected with a giggle.

"Sporting house," Ed agreed. "I was upstairs with Frederica."

"I've never heard of Frederica. Who is she?"

"She was the prettiest senorita you would ever hope to see. Anyway, I was upstairs with her when all of a sudden the door to the room was just kicked open. No warning, no how-do-you-do, no nothing. And there, standing in the doorway, were two of the ugliest galoots you'd ever hope to lay eyes on.

"'Which one are you?' they asked. 'Captain Dunford or Ed Reynolds?' Well sir, when they asked for us that way, I know'd they had to be bounty hunters from Texas."

"What did you do?"

"I told them those warrants had been withdrawn. I told them we weren't wanted men anymore."

"Did they believe you?"

"No."

"What happened?"

"They had the drop on me, so there was nothin' I could do except go with them. I told them that Jake was dead, that he'd died soon after we got out here, but they didn't believe me. They pushed me out into the street in nothin' but my underhauls."

"Ed, how scandalous!" Melanie teased.

"It weren't none too proper, I'll give you that. Especial, what with Fredrica runnin' alongside, ' she warn't wearin' even as much as I had on. She was yellin' at 'em in English and Mexican, cussin' 'em out good 'n proper, tellin' 'em to let me go, but they warn't havin' none of it. They figured to take me out into the center of the street 'n kill me there. That way, you see, they'd have all the witnesses they'd need that I was dead 'n that they was the ones what kilt me. They needed such proof in order to collect the reward. They also figured that Jake would hear about it 'n would try 'n rescue me. When he did, they would catch him too."

"What happened?" Melanie asked, excited.

"That's when your gran'pa stepped in."

"What did Grandpa do?"

"He come out of the bank and seen that them two men had the drop on me. His horse was hitched up in front of the bank 'n your gran'pa pulled his rifle outa the saddle holster. He walked right out into the middle of the street, holdin' that rifle. 'Who are you two men?' he yelled. 'And what are you doin' with my hand?'

"'Stay outa this, mister, unless you wanna get yourself kilt,' one man shouted. The other one raised his pistol toward your gran'pa, but your gran'pa, just as cool as a cucumber, cocked that rifle.

"'Shoot him,' the one holdin' a gun to my head shouted. 'Shoot the old geezer afore he shoots us.'

"The man who was pointin' the gun toward your

gran'pa pulled the trigger, and his bullet carried away your gran'pa's hat. Your gran'pa raised his rifle 'n—get this, girl—he *didn't shoot the one who was shooting at him.*"

"He didn't? What did he do?" Melanie asked in surprise.

Ed was silent for a moment, and Melanie saw that he was swallowing hard. She also saw with surprise that his eyes had misted over.

"He shot the one who was holdin' the gun on me," Ed said. "You see, he risked his own life just to make sure the fella who had a pistol to my head couldn't shoot. Well sir, that gave the other galoot a second shot at him, and the second time he didn't miss. He put a bullet in your gran'pa's shoulder. The gunman was so mad at your gran'pa, 'n so full of hate, that he started toward him, aimin' to finish off the job point-blank. That was when he made his mistake."

"Why?"

"Well sir, the dang fool forgot all about me. There was his partner lyin' in the road beside me, dead, with a loaded gun in his hand. It was easy enough for me. I just picked the gun up and plugged the other fella."

"Good for you."

"Maybe so. But I wound up bein' tried for murder."

"Ed, why would they try you for murder? What you did was in self-defense."

"Accordin' to the law, them two galoots was actin' within their rights to make a citizen's arrest of me 'n your pa. We should'a gone back to Texas with them 'n proved our innocence."

"But they weren't going to take you back. They were going to kill you."

"That was what we argued in court, and your gran'pa hired us a high-powered lawyer to come up from

Phoenix 'n make the case for us. He stuck by us through all of it, 'n after it was over, we was never troubled by those old warrants again."

"And then Mama and Papa were married?"

"Right after that."

"How did Papa come to be foreman of the Turquoise Ranch?"

"When your grandpa retired, Mr. Baker, who was the general manager then, hired your pa on as the new foreman."

"Mr. Baker was general manager of the Turquoise before Les," Melanie said.

"Yes, 'n he was a hell of a lot better'n Garrison could ever hope to be."

"I know Papa liked Mr. Baker. And Grandpa did, too."

Do you remember your gran'pa, girl?"

"Yes, I remember Grandpa," Melanie said. "He died when I was still young, but I remember him." She laughed. "He always carried rock candy in his shirt pocket. I thought it was because he liked candy so much. It was a long time before I realized he was just doing that for me."

"Your gran'pa was a wonderful man," Ed said. "And your mama was a wonderful woman. Put them with your pa and, girl, you gotta turn out good, 'cause there ain't nothin' but good in you."

"I wish Mama were still alive," Melanie said. "Maybe she's up in heaven right now, looking down on us. Do you believe in heaven, Ed?"

"I'm a God-fearin' man, yes," Ed said. "But I gotta tell you that there's some things I've never been able to figure out. And why good people like your gran'pa and your mama have to die before their time is one of those things. Course, I seen that happen a lot durin' the war, so I guess it's been goin' on for all time."

Melanie looked at Ed as he finished the preparations for tonight's stew. He was already bald, and his face showed the signs of living a hard life. To the average cowboy making this drive, the ones who didn't know him, he was nothing but another belly-robber, an ordinary cook. But she knew there was absolutely nothing ordinary about him at all. She was proud to call him her friend. And she was glad to be able to share her wonderful secret with him.

"Ed, why have you never married?"

"I got me a wife. Leastwise, I think I do. I ain't seen nor heard from her in a long, long time."

Melanie's mouth opened in surprise, and she stared at Ed.

"What? You are married? To who? Why have I never seen her?"

"I ain't seen her myself, since long afore you was borned. I left her back in Texas."

"Oh, Ed, I'm so sorry," she said.

"Nothin' to be sorry about," Ed said. "That was a long time ago."

"Why have you never talked about her? You must have been terribly hurt by her"

Ed took the dough Melanie had made and began kneading it. He worked it hard, pounding it with his fists, as if to underscore his story.

"I was hurt all right," he said. "The onliest thing is, I was also a fool. You get wiser when you get older, but generally, especially for an old fool like me, it comes too late."

"Tell me about her. Why did you leave her in Texas? Was she pretty? Did my Papa know her?"

"You ask a lot of questions," Ed said.

"I'm sorry," Melanie said. "You're right, I don't have any business butting into your affairs."

"We was married just before I went off to the war," Ed said. "There was those who told us it would be smarter to wait, but we didn't want to wait. She was sixteen, prob'ly too young to get married 'n settle down, but neither one of us could see that. Oh, we had a big military weddin', don't you know, with flags and bands and pretty uniforms. Course, none of us knew then what we was lettin' ourselves in for. War was somethin' we read about in history books and what we heard the old soldiers talk about. It was flags and uniforms and swords and bands and pretty girls wavin'. Only it warn't nothin' like that a' tall. It was dyin' and screamin', and men with their arms or their legs blowed off. And it warn't all that good for the womenfolk that stayed home, neither. Lots of 'em seen their menfolk die, or come back maimed. Lots of 'em was scared, and when the times got rough, they was hungry, and sometimes the war come right to the home front."

Ed pounded on the dough with his fist. Melanie didn't say anything for a while.

"And some of 'em was lonely," Ed said. There was another beat of silence. "Betsy Mae was lonely. When I come home, I found out just how lonely she was. It was the talk all over the county, how she had took up with a Yankee carpetbagger while I was gone."

"Oh, Ed, how awful," Melanie said.

"I left her soon as I heard. She begged my forgiveness, but I wouldn't have none of it."

"No one could blame you for that."

Ed looked at Melanie, and she saw more pain on his face than she had ever seen in the face of any man.

"I blame me for that," he said. "What I should'a done was just take her with me and leave that place and all the gossip mongers. I should'a just forgot about what happened and made my life with her."

"But surely you don't mean that?"

"Why not?"

"Because she was unfaithful. You had a right to ..."

"What are rights, girl?" Ed asked. "I'm tellin' you true that when two people love each other, they gotta have some bigness about 'em. They gotta know that we are only human, 'n sometimes we make mistakes. And they gotta learn what it's like to forgive."

"If you feel that way, why have you never contacted Betsy Mae?"

"Because the sin I've done her is a lot more'n anythin' she's ever done me. I'm not the one to do the forgivin' now. I'm the one to ask for it. And I would, only I don't know where she is, or how to find her, or even if she is still alive. And if she is, I don't know that I got the nerve to ask her to forgive me."

Ed was quiet for a long moment afterward as he continued to work on the dough. Finally Melanie kissed him on the cheek.

"Thank you, Ed, for sharing with me," she said.

Ed was quiet as she walked away.

20

When Rob told Curly how he felt about Melanie, Curly broke into a big smile.

"So you're tellin' me you think you love her, huh? Next, you'll be 'a tellin' me the sky's blue."

"What do you mean?"

"Well, hell's bells, man, you think I didn't know? All you have to do is look at you when you're around her, 'n it would take a blind man not to see you're nuts about her. But the question is how does she feel about you?"

"I don't know, I didn't ask."

Curly chuckled. "She feels the same way."

"How do you know? Has she said something to you?"

"She don't have to say nothin'. She looks at you just like you look at her. So, tell me, when are you going to ask her to marry you?"

"I'm not going to. She's engaged to Les Garrison."

"Les Garrison is a low-life son of a bitch. The truth is that Melanie, and Jake, too, would be a lot better off if it was you she was 'a marryin', instead of Garrison. The problem is though, if that was to happen, you'd have to find another job somewhere, 'cause he'd likely fire you. Yes, you 'n Big Jake too, 'cause Garrison would fire the both of you. You for takin' his girl, 'n Big Jake for lettin' it happen."

"I guess he would at that," Rob said. "But I wouldn't care, and my guess is, Big Jake wouldn't either."

Curly smiled. "You're right, Big Jake is too much a man to let a little somethin' like that bother him. Course, what Garrison don't know is that when he fires you 'n Big Jake, why, that's the same as firin' me 'n Ed too, 'cause we'll leave just as sure as a gun is iron. And I bet we ain't the only ones that'll be leavin' Turquoise either"

"Now that's one part I don't enjoy," Rob said. "I hate to be the cause of you losing your jobs. And I know how much Melanie loves Turquoise Ranch."

"Don't you worry none about that," Curly said. "Why, Big Jake is that good a foreman that he'll get on somewhere else real pronto, 'n when he does, why, I reckon the rest of us'll have jobs too. He'll see to that. And as far as Melanie lovin' Turquoise Ranch, well, I reckon everyone who has ever lived there loves it. 'Ceptin' maybe Garrison hisself, 'n I don't think he loves anythin' 'bout it, but money 'n power."

"Curly, can you think of anyplace besides the Turquoise where there would be a spread big enough to hire all these people who might lose their jobs?" Rob asked.

"Don't worry about it. Truth to tell, I don't know but what ole Big Jake ain't been saltin' back for a rainy day anyhow. And this is likely to be that rainy day. Who knows? He may start his own ranch 'n we could all work for him."

"Salting back? You mean stealing from the Turquoise?"

Curly looked at Rob with a funny expression on his face.

"I didn't say that," he said. "'N as long as I've know'd Jake, I know that he don't actual have stealin' in 'im a' tall, 'ceptin' what he done when he was back in Texas. 'N that warn't really stealin' none, neither, when you figure out that it was just him gettin' back what was rightly his'n in the first place. Fact is, I don't even know that Garrison's been stealin', neither, though I 'spect he prob'ly is. They's just too many things that don't add up right. I just said I figured Big Jake's been saltin' things back for a rainy day, 'n by that I mean savin' his money he was rightly paid. Anyhow, what difference does it make to you? You surely ain't got no loyalty to Garrison and the Turquoise now, do you?"

"I don't look upon Les Garrison and the Turquoise Ranch as one and the same," Rob said.

"They are as far as *we* are concerned."

"Curly, what if we didn't leave the Turquoise? What if Garrison had to leave instead?"

"Why would Garrison have to leave?"

"He would have to leave if the owner discovered that Garrison was stealing from him."

"Yeah? Well, how is the owner gonna find out?"

"If we found proof and sent it to him, don't you think the owner would fire Garrison? He'd fire Garrison and keep us on."

"'N move Big Jake up to manager 'n me to foreman, I guess," Curly said.

"Maybe."

"No, thank you," Curly said with a surprising amount of emphasis. "That'd be about the low-downest, meanest, most ornery thing I could think of."

"What?"

"Pard, maybe you still got a bit too much Eastern blood in you," Curly suggested. "But they ain't no way you'd ever get me to turn in one of our own to some Eastern dude who don't care enough about his ranch to even come visit it."

"One of our own?"

"Yeah, one of our own," Curly said. "For all that I don't like him, Garrison is still a Westerner, 'n that makes him a better man than the absentee son of a bitch who owns this ranch. Besides, it'd be a pretty low life kind of fella who'd turn another man in just to get a little better treatment for hisself."

"I don't agree with you," Rob said. "If Les Garrison is stealing, he deserves to be punished for it."

"Then let the owner catch him and punish him," Curly said. "I don't want no part o' that."

Up until this conversation, Rob had contemplated telling Curly the truth. He wanted to confess to being the owner of Turquoise Ranch, not only to have someone with whom he could share the news, but also because he hoped Curly would help him get the goods on Garrison. Now he decided it would be best not to tell Curly anything. At least not at this juncture.

THE DRIVE CONTINUED on to the San Carlos Indian Reservation outside Phoenix, and those remaining days were both the happiest, and the most trying days of Rob's life. It was all he could do to keep his feelings away from Melanie, but, he said nothing, and that was particularly hard on him, for he saw her every day at meals.

"I see you got an extra pancake," Curly said as he sat down beside Rob for breakfast.

"You said I should get friendly with the cook's helper," Rob teased. "I'm just following your instructions."

"Speakin' of instructions," Curly said. "Big Jake says we gotta be especial careful for a few days aroun' the cattle. We're comin' into a stretch where we are gonna have a long way between water holes, 'n when the cows start gettin' thirsty, they're awful easy spooked. They could stampede over the least little thing."

"Stampede?"

"Yeah, you ain't never seen one, have you?" Curly asked.

"No, I haven't. Have you?"

"I can't rightly say as I have," Curly admitted. "That is, no full-blowed stampede with as many cows as we got here. I've seen smaller herds panic 'n run, 'n believe me I got out of the way even then. Iffen this herd was to go, we'd have our hands full, I can tell you that."

"Curly, what's the best thing to do if they start to stampede?"

"Get the hell out of their way," Curly said. "The next thing is just to follow 'em, 'n when they get to where you can turn 'em, get 'em started turnin' in a circle. They'll run in a circle until they start gettin' tired, then you can head 'em back in the right direction. But the best thing to do is to keep 'em from stampedin' in the first place."

DESPITE CURLY'S warning and all the good intentions, the herd broke into a stampede that very afternoon. There was no way the cowboys could have prevented it from happening. It was an accidental act of nature which was beyond anyone's control.

There had been no water since early in the morning, and the cowboys had pushed the herd hard to get them through the long, dry passage. The cows were hot, tired, and thirsty. They began to get a little restless, and Rob and the others working around the perimeters were kept busy keeping them going.

Then, at about three o'clock in the afternoon, one of the cows stepped on a dry branch of mesquite. The mesquite popped as loud as a pistol shot, and the noise frightened the cows nearest to the branch. They jumped and started to run and that spread through the rest of the herd. Then, like a wild prairie fire before a wind, the herd ran out of control.

"Stampede! Stampede!"

The call was first issued by one of the cowboys at the front, and it was carried in relay until everyone knew about it.

"Stampede!"

There was terror in the cry, and yet, grim determination too, for every man who issued the cry moved quickly to do what he could do to stop it.

Rob was riding on the right flank when the herd started. Fortunately for him, the herd started toward the left, a living tidal wave of thundering hoof beats, millions of pounds of muscle and bone, horn and hair, red eyes and running noses. They were all welded together as one, gigantic, raging beast.

A cloud of dust rose up from the herd and billowed high into the air. The air was so thick with the dust that within moments Rob could see nothing. It was as if he were caught in the thickest fog one could imagine, but this fog was brown, and it burned the eyes and clogged the nostrils and stung his face with its fury.

Rob managed to overtake the herd, then he rode to

the left, which, before they started running, had been the rear, and he tried to get in front of them to turn them. Rob, like the other cowboys, was shouting and whistling and waving his hat at the herd, trying to get them to respond. That was when Rob got a glimpse, just out of the corner of his eye, of a cowboy falling from his horse. The stampeding cows altered their rush just enough to come toward the hapless cowboy, and he stood up and tried to outrun them, though it was clear that he was going to lose the race.

Rob acted without thinking. He headed for the cowboy, even though it meant riding right into the face of the herd. When he came even with the running man he reached down and picked him up with one hand, using his great strength to lift him as easily as if he were a child. Rob carried the cowboy under his arm and turned his horse to get away from the herd. As he reached the edge, the cows turned again, and Rob and the cowboy he had rescued were safe. Rob set him back down, then rode off to join the others until finally they managed to bring the herd into a big circle. At last the cows slowed their mad dash to a brisk trot, and when they did that the cowboys were able to turn them back in the direction they were supposed to be going. The stampede had at last come to a halt, brought under control by the courage and will of a dozen determined men. An aggregate total of less than eighteen hundred pounds of men were once more in control of over five million pounds of cattle.

Rob was a hero around the campfire that night, and the last vestige of "Eastern tenderfoot" died. Rob was accepted as one of them by even the most reticent of the old hands, for by his action he had won their respect and admiration.

"You've come a long way, pard," Curly said as the two men sipped coffee and stared into the fire after supper. "You know, when I seen you at the railroad station that day, I would'a bet anyone that they was no way you'd ever make a cowman. But the truth is, you are already as good as anyone I ever rode with."

"I had a good teacher," Rob said.

"Now that's a fac', pard," Curly said, beaming under Rob's remark. "That's truly a fac'." Curly stood up and poured the last dregs of his coffee out. "Well sir, me for bed. 'N if you are still listenin' to what your teacher has to say, you'll be doin' the same, I reckon."

"That sounds good to me," Rob agreed.

MELANIE OVERHEARD ALL the cowboys at supper that night as they were telling about Rob's action that day.

"I mean, he reached down 'n plucked up ole' Timmy up like he warn't no more'n a little kid, 'n he tucked him under his arm like a sack o' flour," one of the cowboys said.

"I tell you this, he's the strongest man I ever met," another added.

"What do you say, Timmy?"

"I say if Rob warn't ridin' with us, I'd more 'n likely be dead now. 'N anybody that ever calls him a tenderfoot again, is goin' to have to answer to me."

"You ain't got to worry nothin' about that," another said. "They ain't nobody goin' to ever call him a tender-foot no more."

Listening to all this, Melanie felt a sense of pride in the man she had come to love. And if nothing ever came from her unstated love, she would still feel a proprietary sense of pride.

———

THAT NIGHT, as Rob lay in his bedroll looking up at the stars, he thought of the events of the day, and of his acceptance by the cowboys that night. He thought also of Curly's remark that he was already as good as anyone Curly had ever ridden with. If that was truly the case, then his time of training was over.

It was time he made his identity known.

The only question was *how* was he going to do it?

"You wait till after we deliver them cows," one cowboy said to another as they carried on their conversation not far away from Rob's bedroll. "The first thing I'm gonna do is get me a nice cold bottle of beer. No, two bottles. No, three bottles. And someone soft 'n pretty to drink it with. Then I'm gonna get me a bath."

"Ha," the other cowboy said. "If you don't get yourself a bath first, I guarantee you won't be findin' nobody soft 'n pretty to drink it with."

"And then I'm gonna find me a party," the first one went on, unperturbed by his friend's rejoinder. "A big party with lots o' eats 'n dancin' and pretty women."

A party, Rob thought. Yes, that's what he would do. He would throw a party for all the drovers on this drive, and there at the party, he would announce his identity. Of course, that probably meant that he would not be able to get proof positive that he was being robbed, but that didn't matter. Whatever he had lost thus far was worth it, for the lessons he had learned. He would simply let the ones who stole from him keep their ill-gotten gains, though of course, if it was Les Garrison, he would fire him.

What if it was Jake? Would he fire Jake?

No, he wouldn't fire Jake, because he wouldn't have to. Rob had always been good at reading people, and just as he was certain that Les Garrison was stealing from him, he was equally sure that Jake was not.

WHEN THEY CAME DOWN off the last mountain pass, they could see the main village of the reservation stretched out in front of them. The village consisted of several small houses and tents scattered on both sides of a small creek. The creek which meandered through the village was Cave Creek, a narrow stream that flowed down from the high country, then broke into white water as it bubbled across the tiers of rocks just above the village.

Smoke curled from the roofs of several of the cabins. There were a couple of community corrals for the horses, and there were several dogs. A few of the dogs came out to bark at them.

When they reached the bottom of the pass and started into the village, everyone came out of the houses or away from the wells, which were community gathering places, and came to meet them. A group of children, nut brown from the sun, ran to the village edge and began laughing and running in circles as they formed the vanguard of the impromptu welcoming committee. Many of the adults fell in behind the children and as they walked to the center of the village, they formed a small procession. Then several Indians on horseback came to take charge of the herd, and the cows were taken by the Indians to the private pasture-land of the reservation. At that moment, responsibility for the cows passed from the drovers to the Indians. At first, the cowboys didn't realize that they were finished. Then it dawned on them, and relieved at long last of their duties, they headed for the well, where several of the women and children were drawing water for them. Rob and Curly were among them, and Rob gratefully took a long, cool drink of water and looked around the village.

"Are you looking for Melanie?" Curly asked from the other side of the well. Curly poured some water from the gourd over his head and several of the children, seeing this, laughed at him. Curly drank the second gourd.

"Yes," Rob said.

"She and Ed took the chuck wagon on into Phoenix," Curly said. "He's gonna ship it back up to Flagstaff on the train tomorrow. Fac' is, he 'n Melanie 'n Big Jake will be goin' back by train, too."

"Then I reckon that's how I'll go," Rob said.

"We're supposed to ride back," Curly said. "Lessen we want to pay our own way."

"I'll pay my way. Yours, too, if you want to go."

"Pard, you sure must have more money than sense," Curly said. "Now me, I've got better things to do with my money than spend it on train rides, when I got me a perfectly good horse that can get me back home in no more'n a week."

Big Jake joined the two men then, holding an envelope in his hand. "It seems funny, doesn't it, that all these cows and all this work boils down to what I have in my hand."

"Boss, you gotta be kiddin'," Curly said. "You mean all the money that was paid for these here cows is put into that one envelope?"

"Yes. Well, it isn't cash, it's a bank draft. But it's negotiable, so it's the same thing as carrying cash. I'm going into town now to deposit it in the bank."

"You mean Turquoise Ranch does its banking in Phoenix?" Rob asked. "I would have thought they did their banking in Flagstaff."

"If you would have asked me that question a few weeks ago, I would have agreed with you," Jake said. "But my instructions are not to bring the bank draft home, but to deposit it in the Valley National Bank."

"It would seem to me that if Garrison wanted to be dishonest about that money, hiding it in a Phoenix bank would be a good way to do it," Rob suggested.

"The account is in the name of the Turquoise Ranch," Jake said. "It isn't under Garrison's name."

"Yes, but Garrison has the power of attorney to draw from any working Turquoise account, doesn't he? That would just be a good way to cover up."

"I don't know, maybe you're right," Jake said. "At any rate, it isn't your worry. Or mine either, for that matter. I've done my job. All I want to do now is deposit this draft and get a good night's sleep in a bed, even if it is a hotel bed in Phoenix."

"Boss, you ain't gonna waste time sleepin', are you?" Curly asked. "When there's so many things to do in town?"

"Like what?" Jake asked.

"Like come to my party," Rob said.

Jake, and Curly as well, looked at Rob in surprise. "What party?"

"I'm giving a party," Rob said.

"What kind of a party?" Curly asked.

"A big party," Rob said. "With lots of food, drink and fun. And every drover on this drive is invited to it."

"Rob, you're a damn fool to waste all your money on

a party like this," Jake said. "Hell, man, somethin' like this will cost you more 'n you was paid for the drive."

"It'll be worth it, Jake," Rob said. "Believe me, it'll be worth it."

"There's no way I can talk you outa wastin' your money?" Jake asked.

"I'm afraid not. And I'll be hurt if you don't come."

"Oh, I'll come all right," Jake said with a smile. "If some damn fool is dead set on spendin' all his money on buyin' free food 'n drink for others, then I sure want to get my share. I'll be there, you can count on it."

"Good," Rob said.

Jake started toward his horse. "I guess I'd better go ahead and get on into town. Oh, I suppose Ed and Melanie are included in your invitation?"

"Of course, they are," Rob said

Jake chuckled. "I rather thought they would be. All right, boys, I'll see you two in town."

Rob and Curly watched Jake until he rode away, then Curly looked at Rob and smiled.

"A party, huh?"

"Yep," Rob said, mocking Curly's drawl.

"I tell you what, you're the most perplexin', most confoundin' feller I've ever know'd. Have you actual got enough money to do somethin' like this?"

"I have some money in addition to the wages I've been paid since coming here."

"Well, seein' as you said you come out here for the adventure, I've always sort a' thought that you maybe had more money than sense," Curly said with a chuckle.

WHEN ROB RODE INTO TOWN, he visited the Jones and Meyer law firm.

"Yes, sir, what can I do for you?" a man asked.

"I would like for you to send a telegram to Morgan, Trevathan, and Daigh in Boston. Then, when you get the reply, I would like for you to sign a notarized affidavit, verifying that the telegram is authentic."

"You do understand that there will be a fee for this, above the cost of the telegram?"

"I am well prepared to pay the fee. By the way, I will have to validate my identity by a prearranged code, so I'll write out the message and the code."

"Very well."

Rob accompanied one of the lawyers to the telegraph office, then wrote the message to be sent.

PLEASE IDENTIFY THE SENDER OF THIS TELEGRAM BY THE CODE NAME TEAPARTY RETURN TELEGRAM WITH AUTHENTICATION TO JONES AND MEYER LAW FIRM.

The telegram was dispatched, then, half an hour later there was a reply.

THE FIRM MORGAN, TREVATHAN, AND DAIGH, ADMINISTRATORS OF THE TURQUOIS RANCH BY THIS MESSAGE IDENTIFIES THE IDENTITY OF ROB BARINGER STOP ROB BARINGER THE OWNER OF THE TURQUOISE RANCH.

By these notarized presents, the firm of Jones and Meyer attests to the validity of the message here attached. Given under my hand and seal, Peter Meyer, Attorney at Law.

"Thank you," Rob said as he accepted both the telegram and the notary's validation.

"Are you expecting any trouble in establishing your identity and ownership of the ranch? If so, and you need legal representation, you might consider our firm," Meyer said.

"I am a lawyer, but with no recognition here in Arizona. If it becomes necessary for me to petition the court, I would be glad to use your services," Rob said.

"And it would be our honor to serve you, Mr. Barringer," Meyer replied.

21

"A party? Papa, are you sure Rob said he was going to give a party?"

"That's what he said, all right," Big Jake said. Jake had come to the railroad station to see if Melanie and Ed needed any assistance in shipping the chuck wagon back to the ranch. By the time he got there he discovered that arrangements had already been made. Now he and Melanie were walking down the plank sidewalk of the bustling city, headed toward the Adams Hotel where they would be staying.

"What on earth would make Rob throw a party like that? Why, it would take all the money he's made on this drive," Melanie protested.

"I told him as much," Big Jake said. "But that didn't seem to worry him."

"Well, it might not worry him," Melanie said, "but it certainly does worry me."

Big Jake looked at his daughter with a puzzled expression on his face.

"Girl, what do you mean, it certainly does worry

you?" he asked. "Why would you be worried about what Rob Barringer does with his money?"

"Uh, well, no reason really," Melanie said. "I mean, of course I'm not worried, it's just that…"

"Just what?"

"Nothing. It's just that he's a nice man, but he's so naive, and I hate to think of him wasting his money that way. I mean, who would have thought Rob could be so irresponsible?"

"He's a grown man, darlin', and he can think for himself. And who knows, maybe blowing all his money on a party will teach him a lesson. It's not like he's going to starve to death, he's paid in money and found, as you well know. Besides, we already know that he has a college education. He has been open with the fact that he has come here to be a cowboy for the adventure of it."

"I know," Melanie said. "It's just that he is so different from anyone I've ever met, that I'm not sure he understands what he's doing."

"Darlin', is there somethin' you're not tellin' me?"

"What do you mean?"

"Why have you taken so much more interest in Rob, than you have in any of the others riding for the Turquoise brand?"

Melanie was silent for a long moment. "I… I think I might be in love with Rob."

"Really? When did this happen?"

"I'm not sure, exactly. It just sort of happened."

"Well, Rob's a good man, certainly a better man that Les Garrison, in my opinion," Jake replied. "I hope it works out between the two of you."

"You're all right with it, aren't you?" Melanie asked. "I mean that I've fallen in love with a cowboy?"

Jake smiled. "I know your mama fell in love with a

cowboy, and though our time together was short, it couldn't have been any sweeter"

"That's just what I want it to be like with Rob and me," Melanie said. "And I don't care if he doesn't have anything. A cowboy is good enough for me... if that cowboy is Rob Barringer."

"There's one thing you have to consider, darlin'," Jake said. "If Rob has come here, just for the adventure of it, he may well go back to Boston, when he's done with his adventure. I know that you love Turquoise, how would you feel about leaving it?"

"I... I don't know if I could leave it," Melanie replied. "I hope it doesn't come down to that."

"I'll let you in on somethin'," Jake said secretively.

"What's that?"

"I would be a sight happier about you 'n Rob than I am over you 'n Garrison."

Melanie laughed. "I never did think my engagement to Les had your blessing."

"It's your life, darlin', 'n your decision to make. I didn't figure then, 'n I don't figure now, that I got any say-so in it whatever. But I will tell you that I am a heap happier thinking about you 'n Rob than I was when I thought about you 'n Les."

"Even if it means that I would have to move away from Turquois?"

"I'd hate to see that, but I can't live your life for you. All I can do is hope that you find happiness."

"You're the best father a girl could ever have," Melanie said with a happy smile as she hugged him.

"I just may be at that," Jake said with a humorous laugh.

Melanie was laughing at her father's comment when the two of them walked into the Adams Hotel. There, they saw their names printed on a small blackboard above the message, "Please check with the concierge."

"What do you suppose that's about?" Melanie asked.

"I don't know," Jake said. "Come on, we may as well check with him before we pick up our keys."

"Maybe they don't have rooms for us," Melanie said.

"No, there's no problem with that," Jake said. "I already confirmed our reservations."

A bellboy walked by and Jake reached out and stopped him.

"Excuse me," Jake said, "could you tell me where to find the concierge, please?"

"Yes, sir," the bellboy said. "That's him, right over there, standing by the mailboxes."

"Thank you," Jake said. He led Melanie over to the man the bellboy had pointed out to them, a beefy, bearded man, who was busily poking letters and messages into a wall of post-office boxes.

"Excuse me," Jake said. "You have our names on the board there, asking us to see you."

"Are you Mr. Dunford?"

"Yes."

"I have a message for you," the clerk said. "And you must be Miss Dunford?"

"Yes," Melanie said.

"I have a message for you as well."

"Aren't we the popular ones, though?" Melanie quipped as the manager handed each of them an envelope.

Melanie's was from Rob, and she opened it eagerly.

Dear Melanie,

I am certain that, by now, you have heard of the party that I intend to give tonight. I am going to be extremely busy

during the day taking care of some pressing matters, so I will
be unable to see you until the party. I certainly hope that you
will be there.

Rob

Melanie was pleased that Rob had sent her a personal invitation to his party. She looked over at her father to share her message with him but she was surprised by the expression on his face. Her father was positively ashen faced.

"Papa? Papa, what is it?" Melanie asked. "Is something wrong?"

"What?"

"The expression on your face. Have you received some bad news?"

"No," Jake said absently. He folded the letter and slipped it in his pocket, then he smiled. "No, why do you ask?"

Her father asked the question so innocently, and the smile on his face at that moment seemed so genuine that Melanie began to wonder if she had mistaken the expression earlier. Perhaps it was merely a trick of the light.

"No reason," she said. She held up her letter. "This is from Rob."

"Oh? And what does he have to say?"

"Just that he is going to be taking care of some pressing matters today, but he hopes to see me at the party," she said.

"Where is he now?"

"I don't know. All I know is he said he would see me tonight at the party. Oh, look," Melanie said, pointing to a restaurant which opened off the lobby of the hotel.

"Papa, let's have lunch. It's been a long time since I ate anything without the taste of dust in it."

"You go ahead, darlin', 'n eat without me," Jake said. "I've got somethin' that needs tendin' to."

"Oh, both you and Rob," Melanie said in an exasperated tone of voice. "You are just alike. Both of you have such mysterious tasks to perform on our first day in Phoenix. Well, you just go right ahead. I, for one, am going to enjoy my visit to the city."

Jake smiled and kissed his daughter. "You do that, darlin'," he said. "I'll see you tonight."

Melanie watched as her father walked out of the hotel to take care of whatever mysterious business had come up for him. Then she walked over to the desk to register and get her key.

"My name is Melanie Dunford. I'm with the Turquoise Ranch. I believe you have reservations for my father and me?"

"Ah, yes, Miss Dunford, you have rooms 315 and 317."

"Are both of the rooms the same?"

"Yes."

"Then give me the key to 315. My father will call for his key later."

"Very good, Miss Dunford," the clerk said as he handed her the key. "I hope you have a pleasant stay with us."

"Oh, I intend to," Melanie said, smiling as she took the key.

Melanie walked up the carpeted stairs to the third floor, then down the hall toward Room 315.

The room had a high ceiling and an overhead paddle fan. Melanie turned the fan on, then was rewarded with a brisk, cooling breeze. She left the fan running and went into the bathroom to draw her bath. A few minutes later, she lowered herself down into a tub full of warm, soapy water, and then and only then did it feel as if the long, tiring days of the drive were actually over.

The tub was heaven. She felt as if she could stay in it all afternoon, and she did sit there for way over an hour, until the water went from hot to tepid and finally to cool. Then, reluctantly she stepped out of the tub and walked over to stand at the foot of the bed while she dried herself.

The fan made a tiny hum and *whooshing* sound, and that soothing sound, plus the gentle breath of air thus moved, soon combined to send Melanie off into a most restful sleep.

BIG JAKE SAT on a leather-covered bench in the waiting room of the office of the Arizona Cattlemen's Association. The walls were decorated with polished steer horns, the horns also serving as hat racks. Huge photographs of past and present officers of the Cattlemen's Association also decorated the walls, while against one wall stood a large grandfather's clock. The pendulum steadily swung back and forth as the clock ticked away its measured moments.

"Mr. Dunford," the secretary, a smallish, bald-headed man, said.

"Yes."

"Mr. Cameron will see you now."

"Thank you," Jake said, and walked through the rail gate and back toward the office indicated by Mr. Cameron's secretary.

Cameron stood up as Jake entered, and he smiled and

stuck out his hand.

"Jake," he said, "it's been a long time."

"It has at that, Colonel, it has at that," Jake said.

Cameron chuckled. "I don't hear that very much, anymore," he said. "It's been a long time since anyone called me Colonel."

"Are you uncomfortable with it?"

"No," Cameron said. "Ours may have been a lost cause, but it certainly wasn't a shameful one. I'm proud that I did what I considered to be my duty, and whenever I meet someone who shared that duty with me, I feel good about it. Now, sit down, let's talk."

"I got your note," Jake said. "The one where you said that you wanted to talk to me about the letter I sent you."

"Yes, I did some inquiries as you had requested in your letter, and apparently, your suspicions have some merit. The Colorado Cattle Company has been involved in some questionable deals."

"I was afraid it might be something like that."

"No one has been able to prove them guilty of any wrong-doing," Cameron said as he settled behind his own desk. "But there does seems to be some evidence that Colorado Cattle Company has frequently dealt in stolen cattle, or at least has been accused of such. None of the accusations have been validated, but they have been made by some very reputable people."

Jake sighed. "I just delivered a herd to the Indian reservation. It was a deal Les Garrison worked out with the Colorado Cattle Company."

"Yes, we heard that Garrison had made a sale for the Turquoise Ranch through the Colorado Cattle Company."

"Yes, it was for the Turquoise Ranch," Jake said.

Cameron rubbed his chin. "Jake, I'd be willin' to bet that the owner never sees that money."

"Yes, he will," Jake said.

"Don't count on it."

"He'll see it," Jake said, "because I'm going to send it to him, or them, or whoever it is."

Cameron chuckled. "You mean after all these years, you don't even know who owns the ranch?"

"No. All our dealings have been with a corporation back in Boston, called Morgan, Trevathan, and Daigh," Jake said. "As soon I find some place safe to deposit the money, I'll send it all to the firm in Boston."

"What do you mean safe place? You know the Valley National Bank is a respected bank."

"Yes, but if I deposit the money to the Turquoise Ranch account, Les Garrison will have access to it. And I can't help but feel that he may be involved with the Colorado Cattle Company."

"Yes, I see your point. Well, you could leave the money with us," Cameron said.

"With you?"

"Sure. Sometimes we manage funds for our members. You could just leave the money you get for these cattle with us. That way we could look around, find out who the real owner is and get the money to the right place. Of course, it might well mean your job, in the meantime."

"I've got a feelin' my daughter has already taken care of that," Jake said.

"What do you mean?"

"My daughter was engaged to marry Les Garrison," Jake said.

"You say she *was!* You mean she isn't anymore?"

"No. She met a cowboy on the drive, well, actually she didn't meet him on the drive; she knew him even before. But somethin' must have happened, 'cause it's all changed around. And knowin' Les Garrison as I do, I'm pretty sure he's gonna be a sore loser about it. That probably means I'll be fired as soon as we get back. Rob, too, I'm sure."

"Rob?"

"Rob Barringer," Jake said. "Rob's a finer man than Les Garrison, by far. I don't know that anything will ever come of this. But regardless, she has definitely decided that she doesn't want to marry Garrison, and it's worth losin' my job, just to be knowin' that I won't have that son of a bitch as a son-in-law."

"Well, after this money reaches the real owner, you may find that you haven't lost your job after all. It may be Les Garrison who's out in the cold."

"I figure as much," Jake said. "And that's the way it should be. And I'll not be makin' any profit from this deal."

"Why not? You'd deserve it for getting the goods on Garrison."

"'Cause I won't be doin' this for a reward," Jake said. "I'm not one to profit by another man's problems."

"That's silly, Jake. Even if the other man's problems are of his own doing? After all, Les Garrison is a thief, isn't he?"

"Yes, I reckon he is."

"Then what would be so wrong about taking a reward, if one is offered to you?"

"I lived for a while with paper out on my head," Jake said. "When you got a reward out for you, ever'one you see can make a profit from you if they want. All they have to do is turn you in, or worse, kill you. It makes you feel like an animal."

"Yeah," Cameron said. "I guess I can remember those

days. Some of you got a pretty raw deal when we came back from the war."

"I'm not complainin' or apologizin' for anythin' that ever happened to me," Jake said. "I reckon I cut my own trail, 'n whatever cards life dealt me I had to play with them. For the last twenty years or so I've had a real good life, but the memory of dodging bounty hunters has stayed with me. That's why I don't figure to be a bounty hunter for anyone."

"But this isn't bounty hunting," Cameron protested.

"It's the same thing," Jake said. "I turn Les Garrison in... he loses and I profit. No, sir. I'm willin' to see Les Garrison get what's comin' to him, 'n I'm willin' to see that the owner gets the money that's rightly his. But I'm not willin' to make any gain on the deal."

"Well, a man has to do whatever he considers right, I guess," Cameron said.

"That's always been my creed," Jake said. Jake took an envelope from his jacket pocket. "Here's the bank draft I got at the reservation. Seventy-five thousand dollars. I'd like you to open an account for Turquoise Ranch."

"I'll be glad to," Cameron said. "Listen, would you like to have dinner with my wife and me tonight?"

"I appreciate the offer Colonel, but Rob Barringer is throwing a big party at the Adams Hotel tonight."

"Is that the cowboy you're talking about? The one your daughter's involved with?"

"The same."

Cameron shook his head. "The ballroom at the Adams seems a little expensive for an ordinary cowboy?"

"Whatever he is, Rob Barringer isn't your ordinary cowboy," Jake said.

"It doesn't sound as if he is." Cameron wrote out a

receipt for the bank draft and handed it to Jake. "I'd like to meet him sometime."

"I'm sure you will," Jake said, taking the receipt and putting it in his pocket. "And I want to thank you working with me on this. I may be wrong about Les, and for his sake, I hope I am."

"I think you're doing the right thing, Jake. If there's any chicanery going on, then you're protected. If there isn't, why then there's no harm done."

Jake left the Cattlemen's Association office a short time later, feeling much better than he had when he went in. Not only was he rid of the burden of carrying around a draft for so much money, he was also glad that he had covered himself against any possible repercussions from Les Garrison's cheating.

He felt as if a great weight had been lifted from his shoulders.

22

"I would like to withdraw all the money that's in the Turquoise Account," Garrison said. He was sitting at the desk of the vice-president of Valley National Bank of Phoenix, having arrived by train that morning.

"Very good, sir." The vice-president opened the account book and then opened his cash draw. He withdrew a hundred dollars and handed the money to Les.

"What is this?" Garrison literally screamed the response as he looked at the money.

"I thought you wanted to close out this account and that's the amount of money in this account."

"That can't be! There was a deposit made today—a big one."

"Sir, there's been no deposit made since you opened the account a month ago. I believe it was you who transferred one hundred dollars from a bank in Flagstaff."

Les rose from his seat knocking over the chair. "I'll be back," he said.

Damn! He should have taken an earlier train to Phoenix and been there to meet the herd when it arrived so he could have personally taken receipt of the money. He had managed to take some money off the top of the ranch operations before, but never had he taken this much money. This was seventy-five thousand dollars. What the hell had Jake done with that draft?

The more Garrison thought about it, the angrier he became, then he decided what he was going to do. He went to the City Marshal's office.

"Yes, sir, can I help you?" the marshal asked.

"I want to press charges against Jake Dunford," Garrison said.

"I have to know a little more than a name, mister. Who is this Jake Dunford, and what are you accusing him of?" the marshal asked.

"Jake Dunford is foreman of the Turquoise Ranch, which I'm sure you've heard of. I am Les Garrison, the ranch manager. Dunford brought a herd of cattle down to the San Carlos Indian Reservation. He took possession of a bank draft for the sum of seventy-five thousand dollars. The money was supposed to have been deposited to the Turquoise account in the Valley National Bank in accordance with our agreement, but no such deposit has been made. I believe Dunford has kept the money."

"Do you know where your foreman is now?" the marshal asked.

"I've not seen him but I am assuming he's at the Adams Hotel. Since he doesn't know I've come down from Flagstaff, he would feel no immediate pressure to run away."

JAKE WAS GETTING DRESSED for the party when he heard a knock on his door. Thinking it was Melanie, he smiled and hurried over to open it. "Ready for the par—?" he started to say then seeing Garrison and another man, he got a confused look on his face. "Les, what are you doing here?" he asked.

"Where's the money?" Garrison asked.

"I deposited it."

"You're lying, you made no such deposit. Arrest him, marshal. This son of a bitch just stole seventy-five thousand dollars from me."

"The seventy-five thousand dollars wasn't yours, and I didn't steal it."

"Then where is it?"

"I have no intention of telling you."

"I think you'd better come along with me, Mr. Dunford," the marshal said.

A DOOR SLAMMED at the far end of the hall, and the noise awakened Melanie. It was good that happened, for Melanie had fallen asleep from pure exhaustion, and had she not been awakened she might have slept through the entire night.

Sitting up in bed, she had a moment of confusion. She didn't know where she was, then she remembered that she had lain down right after taking her bath. It was to have been just for a moment, she had thought, but that moment had stretched into hours, and now her room was filled with the shadows of early evening.

Melanie feared that she might have slept through the party, so she walked over to the window and peered through it at the large clock on the front of the bank across the street. The clock said 6:45. She gave a sigh of relief.

She turned away from the window and looked at a package which lay on the dresser. She had gone shopping this morning, even before the arrangements had been made for shipping the chuck wagon back to Turquoise, and she had bought a new dress. Maybe it was a bit extravagant on her part, but she had not brought anything with her on the drive except trail clothes, and she intended to dress up at least one night while she was in Phoenix. When she bought it, she knew nothing about the party; that just turned out to be a happy coincidence.

The basic dress was light blue, and it was designed to fit Melanie's slender figure with a sheath like closeness. It was not a dress that could be worn by many, but for Melanie, it was a perfect fit.

Melanie dressed quickly, then she left her room and walked through the carpeted hallway and down the stairs.

Melanie could hear the sounds of the party even before she got there. Bright lights, conversation and laughter spilled out of the ballroom, welcoming all who might wish to come.

Melanie stopped at the door that led into the room and looked around. As she was late, the party was already in full swing, and the excitement was all it promised to be. There were more than a dozen young women there, though where they came from, Melanie had no idea. They did add life to the party, though, because their bright dresses and flashing earbobs formed collection points around which all the cowboys were gathered.

It wasn't just the Turquoise cowboys, though. There

were all sorts of men present, from the denim- and leather-clad drovers, to the clerks and merchants of the city, fashionably dressed in three-piece suits and gold watch fobs.

A band was playing, but as yet no one was dancing.

Melanie looked for Rob, but she didn't see him. She did see Ed, though, so she walked over to talk to him.

Ed gave a low whistle. "Darlin', you're gonna break every cowboy's heart in this room lookin' like that."

"Do you like the dress?" Melanie asked. "I bought it this morning."

"It's quite a dress," Ed said. "What do you think of the party?"

"There are so many people here," Melanie said, looking around. "I thought it was going to be a party just for us."

"I think it was supposed to be," Ed said. "But these things have a way of growing."

"Is Rob here? I haven't seen him," Melanie said.

"I haven't seen him either, but seeing as it's his party, I'm sure he'll be here sometime."

Ed had no sooner spoken the words, when Rob arrived.

"Well, speak of the devil," Ed said with a smile.

"Rob!" someone called. "This is some party, glad you could make it."

Rob laughed. "Well, since I'm paying for it, I thought it might be a good idea for me to show up."

Rob came over to speak to Melanie and Ed, and they were visiting, when Curly came into the room.

"Ah, there's Curly," Ed said.

"Look at the expression on his face. Something's wrong," Melanie said.

"Curly, over here," Ed called.

Curly hurried through the crowd to Rob, Ed, and Melanie. Unlike the other cowhands, Curly was still wearing his trail clothes and pistol belt. When he arrived, both Rob and Ed could see what Melanie had seen.

"What is it, Curly? What's wrong?" Ed asked.

"Jake's in jail," Curly said.

"What?" the explosive response came from all three of them.

"Why is he in jail?" Melanie asked in a frightened voice.

"I'll tell you why he's in jail. Because that son of a bitch Garrison had him arrested."

"For what?" Ed asked.

"He says Jake stole the money that was paid for the cattle."

"That's impossible," Melanie said. "Dad would never do anything like that."

"I'm going to go bail him out," Rob said.

"Oh, Rob, after all the money you've spent for this party, I'm afraid you won't have enough to bail him out."

"Let's wait and see what the bail is."

"I'm going with you," Melanie said.

"Me, too," Ed said.

"Come with me. I saw where they put him," Curly offered.

The four of them hurried down the main street toward the jail. When they stepped inside, they saw Les Garrison.

"Les, what's going on here?" Melanie asked. "Curly said you had my dad arrested. Why?"

"I had him arrested because he stole seventy-five thousand dollars from me," Garrison said.

"From you? I thought that seventy-five thousand dollars belonged to Turquoise Ranch," Rob said.

"As far as anyone here is concerned, I *am* Turquoise Ranch," Garrison said, arrogantly.

"How much is bail?" Rob asked. "I'd like to bail him out."

"Bail hasn't been set, but I expect it will be at least a hundred dollars," the marshal said.

Rob took out his billfold, and removed two one-hundred-dollar bills. "This should cover it," he said. "If it is less, I'll come back and get my change."

"All right," the marshal said, and getting up from his desk, he retrieved the key to the cell, then stepped into the back.

Melanie, Ed, and Curly were looking at Rob in shock.

"Who the hell do you think you are coming in here and bailing out a thief like Jake Dunford?" Garrison asked.

"I don't believe Jake stole the money," Rob said.

"Well, he sure as hell didn't deposit it in the bank," Garrison said with an angry snarl.

"How could he? He hasn't been back to Flagstaff yet."

"He was supposed to make the deposit in the bank, here."

"Why here? Turquoise doesn't have an account here."

"They do now. And what do you have to say about what I do?"

"Don't you need such a transaction to be authorized by Morgan, Trevathan, and Daigh?" Rob asked.

Garrison's expression changed. "And just how is it that you know about Morgan, Trevathan, and Daigh?"

At that moment the city marshal returned with Jake. "He's all yours," he said.

"Dad!" Melanie called out, and she ran into her father's arms.

"You're fired!" Garrison shouted. "All of you are fired!"

"That's fine by me," Curly said. "I don't want to work for a son of a bitch like you, anyway."

"What will we do now?" Melanie asked in a frightened tone.

"May I make a suggestion? Let's go back to the party that I've already paid for," Rob said.

"Yeah, why not?" Ed replied. "We can decide what we're gonna do from there."

"You're just out on bail, you son of a bitch. You can't get away with stealing all that money," Garrison called out as Jake and the other four left the jail house. "I'll see you hang!"

"Dad, where is the money?" Melanie asked as they were walking back to the hotel.

"I deposited it. I just didn't put it in the bank Les wanted me to use."

"But if you deposited it, why didn't you tell him where it is? Then he wouldn't accuse you of stealing."

"Because I deposited it to a Turquoise account. And if Les knew where it was, he'd be authorized to withdraw the money. And if he did that, I don't think the owners, whoever they may be, would ever see one cent of the money."

"I think you did the right thing," Rob said.

Jake nodded. "Thanks, I appreciate you saying that. You're 'bout the smartest man I've ever known, and it makes me feel good that you believe that."

The party was still going in full swing when they returned, and Rob held out his hand to Melanie. "Let's dance."

"I thought you'd never ask," Melanie replied, with a smile.

They danced to two more tunes, then as they separated after that dance, Rob smiled at Melanie. "Hold on here for a moment, I need to make an announcement."

"An announcement? What sort of announcement? Rob, don't you think we should talk about this before you make our engagement public? Especially as there are so many people here that we don't even know."

"Don't worry, Melanie, you won't be embarrassed," Rob said, with an enigmatic smile.

Melanie watched, filled with nervous curiosity, as Rob walked over to the band and said something to them. Instead of a song, the band played a riff, that got everyone's attention. When all looked toward the band, they saw Rob standing there, holding his arms up.

"Friends, if you'll give me your attention, I have an announcement to make."

"An announcement? What sort of announcement?" someone called.

"Well, maybe if you'll just shut up, he'll tell us," another said.

"Go ahead, Rob," Jake said.

"What's his announcement?" Curly asked Melanie. "He's not gonna say somethin' about you 'n him, is he?"

"I don't really know," Melanie said. "He told me he was going to make an announcement, and that I wouldn't be embarrassed by it, but I don't have any idea what this is about. I guess I'll just have to listen like everyone else."

The crowd grew quiet then, not only out of respect for Rob's wishes, but also because they were curious as to what the announcement was going to be.

"As you know," Rob started, "I've spent the last several

weeks working on the Turquoise Ranch. It isn't by accident that I came to work here. I came to Turquoise Ranch by design, because I wanted to gain some valuable first-hand experience and knowledge of the business of ranching.

"I've learned a great deal from Jake, from my friend Curly, as well as from the rest of you. I don't believe I am the same man who arrived here, fresh from Boston, last spring."

"I'll have to confess that your feet aren't quite as tender," Curly called out, and the others laughed.

"No," Rob agreed. "My feet aren't quite as tender, nor am I quite the babe in the woods I once was. That's why I feel I am ready to quit being a cowboy…"

"Quit being a cowboy? Rob, no, you aren't giving it up, are you? Are you leaving us?" someone called.

Melanie gasped when he announced he was going to quit being a cowboy. Did this mean he was going to return to Boston? She loved ranching, and the West, and she had thought that he shared some of that love.

Rob smiled and held out his hands, again asking for quiet.

"Now wait a minute," he said. "I didn't say anything about leaving. I just said I was going to quit cowboying."

"What are you gonna do?"

"What I'm about to say is going to surprise you, but, I have a telegram from the firm of Morgan, Trevathan, and Daigh, in Boston, and from the Jones and Meyer law firm here in Phoenix, I have a notarized certificate as to the authenticity of the telegram."

"Get on with it, pardner, what's the telegram about?" Curly asked.

"It says that I'll be running my own ranch," Rob said.

"*Your* ranch? What are you talking about? Have you

bought a ranch?" Jake asked. He smiled, "Seein' as me 'n Ed, 'n Curly was just fired, would you be interested in hiring us?"

"I don't have to hire you, you are all already hired. It's Les Garrison who is fired."

"Rob, what are you talking about? What ranch do you own?" Curly asked, still puzzled by the announcement.

Rob held up the telegram. "I own Turquoise Ranch," he said.

There were gasps of surprise from almost everyone present.

"I know'd it!" Curly said. "I know'd damn well they was somethin' different about you. Hell, you ain't like nobody I ever met before."

"What was you doin', spyin' on us?" one of the cowboys asked.

"There ain't no call for that, Dusty. I got to know Rob, uh, I mean Mr. Barringer real good, 'n I can say I ain't never know'd nobody no better," Curly said.

"Thanks, Curly, and it is still Rob. To all who work on the ranch, it's still Rob."

"Are we goin' to have to put up with a lot of changes?" another cowboy asked.

Rob smiled. "Well, there's one change I'm going to make right away. As I said a moment ago, Les Garrison is fired."

Everyone present cheered at the prospect of Garrison being fired.

After the announcement, Rob came back to rejoin Melanie, who was looking at him with a shocked expression on her face.

"Rob, why didn't you tell me?" she asked.

"I fell in love with you, Melanie. And I hoped to win

your love, not because I owned the ranch, but because you loved me, for myself."

Melanie smiled. "Well then, you succeeded, Rob Barringer, because I absolutely fell in love with you even when I thought you were..."

"Nothing but a cowboy?" Rob asked.

"Oh, sweetheart, you never were 'nothing but' anything. You are the 'most somethin' I've ever known." She kissed him and those close enough to see, applauded.

The party continued with dancing, food, and drink. Then, to get a breath of fresh air, Rob, Melanie, Jake, Ed, and Curly stepped outside.

"I'll tell you this," Curly said. "You might be the ranch owner, but in my opinion, you're also the best cowboy on the entire ranch."

"I appreciate that Curly, and..."

"You son of a bitch, you can't fire me! I'm going to kill your sorry ass!" The loud shout, coming from the middle of the street, was followed by the sound of a gunshot. Rob let out a grunt of pain and fell to the ground.

"Rob!" Melanie shouted in horror, as she dropped to her knees beside him.

Another shot split the night air, but when Melanie looked up, she saw that Curly was holding a smoking pistol in his hand, and Les Garrison was lying in the road.

"Let me through!" someone said, and one of the guests of the party, who identified himself as a doctor, knelt beside Rob, and began examining his wound.

"It's not that bad," he said. "It's a shoulder wound.

Let's get you down to my office and I'll get you fixed up good as new."

"What about the other feller, Doc?" someone asked.

"The doc ain't goin' to do him no good," someone who was standing over Les Garrison's body called back to them. "This feller is dead. He was hit right between the eyes."

"Melanie?" Rob said in a strained voice.

"What is it?" Melanie asked, bending closer to hear him.

"Will you marry me?"

Melanie laughed. "This is a fine time to ask a girl that question, but you know my answer. Yes, I'll marry you."

She helped him up and when she did, she kissed him as Jake, Curly, Ed, and the others cheered and clapped.

A LOOK AT: IRON HORSE

BY ROBERT VAUGHAN

FROM NEW YORK TIMES BEST-SELLING AUTHOR ROBERT VAUGHAN COMES A WESTERN FICTION NOVEL OF DETERMINATION, OBSTACLES, AND LOVE.

Gabe Hansen is determined to build a railroad from Albuquerque to the Pacific Ocean, but first, he must deal with two major adversaries.

One is Bernardo Tafoya, a Mexican who does all he can to prevent the railroad from coming through land that his family holds by virtue of an old Spanish land grant. The other obstacle to the railroad is Peter Van Zandt, son of Emory Van Zandt, the financier who is backing the railroad. Peter wants to get control of the railroad for himself.

Makenna O'Shea is a beautiful young woman who becomes a surprisingly strong ally, falling in love with Gabe in the process. Makenna is forced to make a decision that saves the railroad, but at the expense of her relationship with Gabe.

AVAILABLE NOW

ABOUT THE AUTHOR

Robert Vaughan sold his first book when he was 19. That was 57 years and nearly 500 books ago. He wrote the novelization for the miniseries *Andersonville*. Vaughan wrote, produced, and appeared in the History Channel documentary *Vietnam Homecoming*. His books have hit the NYT bestseller list seven times. He has won the Spur Award, the PORGIE Award (Best Paperback Original), the Western Fictioneers Lifetime Achievement Award, received the Readwest President's Award for Excellence in Western Fiction, is a member of the American Writers Hall of Fame and is a Pulitzer Prize nominee. Vaughn is also a retired army officer, helicopter pilot with three tours in Vietnam. And received the Distinguished Flying Cross, the Purple Heart, The Bronze Star with three oak leaf clusters, the Air Medal for valor with 35 oak leaf clusters, the Army Commendation Medal, the Meritorious Service Medal, and the Vietnamese Cross of Gallantry.